WHITE GOLD IN THE CASSIAR

Books by William G. Crisp

OOK-PIK
WHITE GOLD IN THE CASSIAR

WINNER OF BOYS' LIFE
DODD, MEAD PRIZE COMPETITION

WHITE GOLD
in the
CASSIAR

William G. Crisp

DODD, MEAD & COMPANY
New York   1955

Library of Congress Catalog Card Number: 55-9828

Printed in the United States of America
by the Vail-Ballou Press, Inc., Binghamton, N.Y.

Dedicated to
the Four Scotts of Dunbar

CONTENTS

WHITE GOLD IN THE CASSIAR

1

INTO THE DEVIL'S CLUB

SCOTT HALIBURTON stood on the upper deck of the river boat *Chutine*. He could see the mountains of the Alaskan panhandle only as vague black shapes shrouded in rain clouds. The tidal flats of the Stikine estuary had slipped into the mists astern.

Ahead, beyond the Coast Range, lay the remote northwestern corner of Canada. It was known as the Cassiar and Scott was going to spend the summer in the heart of the Cassiar Mountains, at his father's gold mine on Osprey Creek.

Scott glanced at the stocky youth beside him. He hadn't expected to find anyone so close to his own age as Jack among the passengers. Scott still had one more year of high school ahead of him. Jack Birk was bound for his first job. He was starting as a clerk at the Hudson's Bay fur post at Telegraph Creek. That would be the end of the *Chutine*'s voyage, because the narrow canyons above the post rendered the Stikine unnavigable.

Scott found himself wishing that Jack would be coming

all the way with him—across the trail over the Arctic Divide and down the Dease River to Osprey Creek. The two boys were drawn together, not only by their youth, but by the discovery that they both had problems to face.

Jack's wages would supplement the small pension of his widowed mother. But he wanted to do more than that—to be able to send enough money home to help his sister start her nurse's training.

"So that," said Jack, "is why I'd like to find gold in this country."

Scott gave him a wry smile. "Just finding gold doesn't make you wealthy. It might be just a rich pocket that peters out. Or, if the gold has to be washed out with hydraulic monitors, as it does at Osprey Creek, it costs thousands of dollars to freight in equipment. Even then, there may not be enough water power to run the monitors. Placer gold mining is a gamble."

He should know, Scott told himself. Hadn't his father told him that if Osprey Creek didn't start producing this year, all the money and work he'd put into it during the past three years would be lost? That would mean Scott would have to give up any idea of starting University—let alone his dreams of post-graduate training in geology.

An icy raindrop spattered on Scott's close-cropped fair hair. He shuddered. "Let's go down to our cabin," he suggested.

"Smart idea—I'll carry your bedroll." Jack hesitated with the bundle poised on his shoulder. "Say! How come your dunnage is still on deck? It hasn't been out of your sight since it came on board at Wrangell."

Scott shrugged. "No special reason. I guess I've been too interested in the river." He started to hoist up his duffel bag. A sudden look of concern flashed across his face. "Hey! Wait a sec!" He dropped the bag on the deck and pummeled it with his fists.

Jack's brown eyes twinkled. "What's up?" he asked, setting the bedroll down again.

Scott fumbled with the drawstring of the bag. "A granny knot!" he said with disgust. "I sure didn't tie this!" He worked the cord loose and thrust his arm into the bag. "My sack of rock samples is missing! I'm dead sure I packed it last thing before I came ashore from the coast steamer. By golly! One of those loafers who were hanging around the dock at Wrangell must have pinched them."

Jack looked puzzled. "Were they valuable?"

"Only to me. I'll have to start all over again now and it will take time to get another collection together." Scott's expression changed momentarily. A quick smile flashed across his face. "Say! There were some bits of iron pyrites—Fool's Gold—anyone who just took a quick look might have mistaken them for high grade gold quartz."

His friend chuckled. "Wouldn't you like to see his face when he finds he's been fooled by Fool's Gold?"

But Jack's remark fell on deaf ears as Scott pondered the mystery in silence. It must have been somebody on the dock who had stolen his rock collection. No doubt about that, he decided. But why had they picked his bag? Because it was labeled "Osprey Creek Mine"?

"Wait a shake! Keep your eye on things, will you?" he asked Jack. "I'm going up to the pilothouse and report this to the skipper."

Scott walked forward and knocked gently at the door of the wheelhouse. When it opened, he stood shyly, feeling all arms and legs under the scrutiny of Captain Dan's steel gray eyes. He had heard stories of the captain's uncertain temper, but now he dared to hope that he had found the skipper in a good mood.

"Come in—you can sit up on that stool," the captain invited.

Scott's spirits soared. He was starting to whistle as he stepped inside. But one step was as far as he got. Captain Dan's hand suddenly clamped on his shoulder. He found himself spun around and pushed back on deck.

"Better go below until you learn how to behave. You confounded little . . . little . . ." The captain seemed to be searching for the right word. "Confounded little Jonah," he growled and slammed the door.

Dazed by the suddenness of his undignified exit, Scott hesitated for a few seconds at the fore rail. From the freight deck below he could hear the muffled voices of two of the deck hands. "Did'ja see all this pipe for Osprey Creek? Be worth its weight in gold by the time the freight's paid on it."

The voice that replied was coarse and cynical. "Bah! The ruddy gold they ship out won't weigh much anyway. Oh well—no skin off our noses. Every two or three years some outfit tries to work one of the creeks—and it's freight going into the Cassiar that pays our wages."

Words his father had spoken became a dismal chorus in Scott's mind, "If the mine doesn't pay this year . . .

if the mine doesn't pay . . . if . . ." He suddenly became conscious of a steady splatter of rain. Shivering, he started back aft.

He found Jack talking to Gee-gee, the little gray-bearded wrangler who claimed he owned the best string of pack horses in the Cassiar.

"Whistlin' in the pilothouse, I take it," Gee-gee boomed in his surprisingly deep voice. "You shouldn't ha' done that. Cap'n Dan thinks it's mighty unlucky. Sure gets him riled up."

Scott looked sheepishly at Jack. "Guess I'll tell the skipper later. He didn't seem. . . ." A shrill blast on the *Chutine*'s air whistle interrupted him.

Gee-gee rumbled, "We're pulling into the Boundary. We'll be there for about an hour while the Canadian Customs officer checks the cargo lists. Whatever you have to tell the captain, you'll have lots of time. It'll be a long three days' drag upstream to Telegraph Creek, even though the water is droppin' fast."

Scott shouldered his bag and followed Gee-gee down the companionway to the living quarters below. At the bottom, the boy hesitated for a minute or two, his eyes blinking in the dim light. He could feel Jack pressing to pass him, but the old wrangler stubbornly blocked their way.

"A lot of folks are gettin' steamed up about these airy-planes." The old man had something he wanted to get off his chest. "I figure it'll be a long time before they do me out of business, though. Horses don't have to wait for clear weather before they take off."

"Sure—sure," Scott didn't argue with him. Looking over the wrangler's shoulder, he saw one of the cabin doors open at the far end of the corridor. Somebody came out and moved into the deeper gloom at the opposite side. Then there was a brief flash of daylight and the figure disappeared—apparently through a door leading outside.

Almost at the same time, a bell clanged and the rumble of the gas engines stopped.

"I'll see you boys later." Gee-gee's voice sounded deeper than ever in the sudden hush. He turned out of Scott's way and disappeared through the door of the dining saloon.

Scott felt Jack push past him. "Come on," he said. "Our cabin's down at the far end."

"It . . . it can't be this one," Scott stammered. "Somebody just came out of this door."

"Sure! This is our cabin," Jack replied lightly. "See— here are my suitcases. I haven't even unstrapped them yet. You must have been seeing things."

"Not on your life! It was too dark to see much, but whoever it was came out of this cabin and went through that door—there!"

Jack opened the door Scott had pointed out. "This opens onto the stern. No one could have gone this way unless he jumped into the river . . . or unless he walked around the guard rail."

". . . and jumped ashore," added Scott. "Jack, grab your hat and lock the cabin door. If you're not afraid of the rain, what say we go after him and see what goes on?"

The two boys slipped out through the stern door and edged along the guard railing. The boat was nosed into a clay bank so that before they came opposite the dining saloon amidships they were able to jump ashore and scramble up to a clearing about level with the upper deck.

"Customs man just going aboard now," Jack whispered, nodding his head towards the gangway at the bow. He motioned Scott into the shelter of a clump of brush. "Guess nobody saw us. I don't see any footprints on the bank except our own. You must have been dreaming."

Scott clutched him by the arm. "The heck I was! Keep out of sight—Look! We didn't notice there was a ladder to the upper deck just beyond that door we came through. There he is! Just passing the exhaust stack now."

"That's Schnider—the chap they call Gold Brick," Jack murmured. "He's a mining promoter, he told me. Must do well at it by the looks of the expensive high-topped leather boots and outdoor clothes he wears."

"Yes—I was talking to him too," Scott said. "All I've got against him is that he insists on calling me 'Scotty.' Must admit he didn't sound like the type who'd prowl in a fellow's cabin. If I did see him coming out of our cabin, maybe he'd just mistaken the number."

He looked around curiously. The Customs office was at the far side of a clearing, ringed by giant cottonwoods. "Hi!" he exclaimed. "Here's some sort of a trail. Are you game to do a little exploring, now we're here?"

"Okay, lead the way."

They trudged in silence along the trail, which soon became no more than a narrow tunnel through thick tangles of devil's-club and salmonberry bushes. A dank, swampy smell rose up from the sodden earth which was hidden beneath a dense covering of salal and giant ferns. It seemed to grow darker as they pushed on.

After they had gone about a hundred yards, Scott stopped and looked at his watch. There was no sound but the rustle of raindrops trickling from leaf to leaf. "Shall we go on for another ten minutes?" he whispered.

"Gosh!" Jack murmured cautiously. "I don't know. This jungle is tougher than anything I've ever tackled."

Actually the undergrowth was thicker and ranker than Scott had bargained for, but he didn't like to admit it. "Come on!" he urged. "You should have seen the brush we hiked through at Scout camp last summer. I'll show you how to get through devil's-club."

The forest was strangely hushed as they pushed on. The salmonberry bushes gave an almost inaudible rustle as they brushed past them. The boys' footsteps made only faint squelches in the mud. Scott glanced around as razor sharp thorns of devil's-club caught on his jacket and whipped backwards. He saw Jack throw up his arm to ward off the lash of the greenish-brown shoot. Neither of them spoke. Scott shrugged and resumed the stealthy trek. . . . Five minutes later he came to a sudden stop. This looks like the end of the trail, he thought, as the dripping silence of the forest held him in its spell.

2

BEYOND THE GLACIERS

A FALLEN tree lay across the boys' path. It was an aged giant of a cottonwood with its twisted roots reaching toward the sky at the left side of the trail.

Scott turned to Jack with a smile that meant, "Well —what do you think of that? This is the size of our West Coast trees." But he didn't utter the words—it seemed a long time since either of them had spoken. Now that they were standing still, there wasn't even the swish of the brush nor the soft plop and squelch of their boots in the mud. There was only the rustle of the leaves, tilting to rid themselves of the raindrops.

Scott hoped Jack would say something. Suddenly he wanted to hear the sound of a voice, to open his own mouth and talk about something. About the trees, the rain, the river—about anything.

But Jack merely lifted his eyebrows in an expression that meant, "Sure—it's a big tree," and waved his arm up toward the roots.

Scott nodded in reply. Okay—they would climb the roots

9

and have a look around—it would be something to look over the tops of the devil's-club. Jack climbed on to the butt of the log. Grasping one of the upturned roots, he reached down to give his friend a hand up the slippery, mud-coated ascent. He tightened his grip as Scott fumbled for a new foothold, and gasping for breath, landed on the tree trunk.

A rising crescendo of sound, a splintering crash, and the root to which Jack had been clinging gave way. It was Scott's turn to hold Jack steady as the startled pair listened to the series of muffled thuds that followed.

Then there rose a roar that made Scott catch his breath. He looked beyond Jack and saw a silvery-brown head swaying from side to side, almost level with the top of the big tree trunk. It was a bear, reared up on its hind legs, its lips drawn back in a snarl that disclosed long yellow fangs. Its narrow pig-eyes were blinking straight at these unexpected intruders. Slowly the animal's bewilderment gave way to mounting fury.

Suddenly Scott's body lost every vestige of warmth, and his rain-soaked clothes felt wet and clammy. Perhaps it was only for a few seconds that he looked into those glaring eyes, perhaps it was for only a fraction of a second. And then he was moving—running along the log.

"Jack—a grizzly—climb a tree!"

From the devil's-club below them came a growling and crashing. Glimpses of a mass of brown fur appeared through the quivering underbrush. A huge paw reached up with long yellow claws.

Here was a tree now—close enough to the log for Scott to reach its lowest branch. Jack's hands clasped below his foot to boost him up. Then Scott was clinging to a branch and reaching down to give a hand. A twig caught Jack's battered felt hat and sent it spinning along the log. The hairy paw was suddenly drawn back. There was a silence, a thud, and the crashing in the underbrush began again. But this time it moved in the opposite direction, grew fainter and fainter and died away.

"Wow!" Jack brushed the back of his hand across his forehead. "Didn't seem very friendly, did he?"

"I'll say he didn't—but he seems to be in a big rush to get away now." Scott found he was able to laugh. He could hear the rustling of the forest again. He felt a warm glow creeping over him, and the sensation of clammy dampness disappeared. Up in the tree, ten feet or so above the devil's-club, they seemed to have emerged from deep gloom to a soft, green brightness. Just below him, raindrops trickled like glass beads over Jack's brown hair.

"Well—guess there's no need to sit here any longer with the rain running down the back of my neck." Jack started to slide down to the next branch.

"Jack! Don't go down yet! Listen!" Something was crashing through the brush again.

"Suffering catfish! That's coming from the other direction—there's one between us and the river. What do we do now?" Jack started to climb up again as the noise grew closer.

"Holler at the top of your voice—shout, scream, kick your feet on the trunk. Make all the noise you can," Scott yelled.

For two solid minutes they filled the woods with a mighty and weird noise. The moment they stopped, there was silence. No echoes came back through the quivering leaves. Then a branch snapped almost directly beneath them, and a voice boomed, "What in tarnation is goin' on up there?"

"Gee-gee!" the boys shouted in a perfect duet. Quickly they slid down from the tree. No more conversing in whispers and sign language now. Gee-gee climbed up onto the log, and Jack recovered his hat from the devil's-club on the other side.

Quickly, nervously, Scott's words spilled out as he told Gee-gee the whole story about the bear. When he was finished, he waited while the wrangler examined the tracks in the wet earth below the up-tilted roots—long, narrow pad marks with the imprint of five pointed claws ahead of them. What would Gee-gee say? That they had been foolish to climb a tree? That all you needed to do to make a grizzly run was to wave your arms and yell at him? He remembered the two bears in the salmonberry patch at camp last summer. They ran away—but they were black bears.

"Thunderation!" Scott felt that the great tree trunks must be vibrating in tune with Gee-gee's voice. "You sure were a couple of crazy young mavericks; lighting out like that into the worst grizzly country along the river. Soon as the Customs man came on board to check the passenger list, I had a hunch what was goin' on, and 't'wasn't hard to pick up your trail. Reckon you were sneakin' along quietly. Looks as if that bear was havin' a snooze and you just about stepped on him."

Scott stroked the back of his head and shot a glance at Jack. He supposed he looked even more sheepish than Jack did. And rightly so, he thought—the expedition had been his idea in the first place.

"You should have made lots of noise to make sure you weren't goin' to walk into trouble. You could hear me comin'—couldn't you? No bear would have been waitin' around for me to arrive."

Gee-gee was leading the way back along the trail now. Falling in behind Jack, Scott chewed at his lower lip and thought how stupid he had been. The trio strode along in silence for a few minutes. Evidently, Scott decided, Gee-gee knew there was no danger of running into any bears now. And then a glowing brightness ahead of them showed him that they were almost back to the clearing.

"Tell you one thing, though." Gee-gee suddenly turned and faced the boys. "If you'd started to run back up the trail, he might have taken after you. Can't tell what a grizzly is goin' to do when you surprise him like that. Yes, sir—when you lit out for that tree, you sure had the right idea."

Scott grinned. So they hadn't been complete fools. They had done the best they could under the circumstances—Gee-gee had said so. He felt a warm glow inside himself, and the lowering sky overhead seemed almost bright as they emerged from the forest.

Crossing the clearing, Scott could see the *Chutine*'s pilot house appearing above the riverbank. He pictured himself in the after cabin below, swapping yarns with men who knew the Northland's rivers and forests.

"Hey, Gee-gee! Won't those fellows on the boat get a kick out of it when we tell them what happened?"

The wrangler wheeled around again. "Take my advice and don't tell them anythin'. If you do, they'll just laugh and say you were another pair of greenhorns with a bad case of 'buck fever.' Won't help if I say anythin'. 'Just another of his bear stories,' they'd say. They never would believe me."

"Well, if that's the way it is . . ." Disappointment held Scott's words back.

But Jack's quiet laugh cheered him up. "Don't look as though you've lost your best friend. We can keep this a top-secret between the three of us. We'll clam up and let that gang on the boat do some guessing. Could be we'll get a kick out of it."

"That makes good sense," Gee-gee rumbled.

"Okay with me, I promise not to say a word." Scott was smiling now.

The Customs man, standing in the doorway as they passed his office, waved them on with a grin. Gee-gee roared, "There y'are, Birk and Haliburton—told you I'd soon round them up."

The three hurried on down the slippery clay path to the landing. The *Chutine*'s engines were coughing puffs of bluish smoke from the exhaust pipes near the water line at the stern. The captain had let down one of the pilot house windows and was leaning with his elbows on the sill.

"What the muddy thundering blazes has been going on?" he bellowed. "I'm running a freight and passenger service—not a school picnic."

"Hold your hosses, Cap'n!" Scott supposed the skipper would be more furious than ever after Gee-gee said that. But they were entering the lower-deck now, and could only judge by the three short blasts on the whistle how the captain felt. The staccato "beeps" came in rapid succession, like exclamation marks following the skipper's words.

By the time the boys reached their cabin, the engines were running full speed ahead and the door was rattling and jingling with the vibration. They didn't waste any time changing into dry clothes. Appetizing wafts were coming from the galley, putting a sharp edge on their appetites. They hurried along the corridor to the dining saloon, hardly noticing the hot, oily reek of the engines.

Nobody paid any attention to their arrival. Everyone appeared to be too busy eating to speak. Even Captain Dan didn't look up as they slipped into the only two vacant chairs, which were on opposite sides of the circular table.

Scott soon discovered that you didn't even have to say: "Pass the sugar, please," or anything like that. There was a revolving stand in the center of the table, and you just reached out and twirled it around until whatever you needed came into view.

He gave the stand a gentle twist and stopped it as the pepper and salt swung around. Golly! It turned easily—

must have ball bearings. He salted and peppered his soup and returned the shakers to their places. He could see Jack, across the table, reaching toward the stand. Their eyes met and they grinned at each other.

Scott gave the turntable a rapid twirl—probably it would go around two or three times before Jack could stop it. It started to spin like a huge top and there was a burst of laughter from the other side of the table. Leaning to one side, Scott could see that the whirling motion had shot a bottle of catsup off the stand. A young man had caught it deftly before it had a chance to spill.

"Stur-r-ike three! You're out!"

Scott slumped low in his chair and stared at his plate. He felt his ears burning and he was sure that his face must be as red as the catsup. Strike three it was—the third stupid thing he'd done since he came aboard.

"That there was a demonstration of centrifugal force." No mistaking Gee-gee's deep voice.

"The same principle we use for panning gold. You twirl the pan back and forth like this," Gold Brick said, holding an empty soup plate by both hands. Scott raised his eyes and stared, fascinated by the sight of the huge nugget in Gold Brick's ring describing figure eights in the air.

"Nuts!" A disgusted comment came from across the table. "Gravity—that's what separates the gold from the gravel."

A loud gargle and the sound of a heavy crockery cup clinking on a saucer came from Scott's right. Good grief! Captain Dan! What was the skipper thinking of his latest blunder? Certainly he was managing to get in Dutch with the captain. He'd have to face up to him, though—no chance of keeping out of his sight for three days on a boat the size of the *Chutine*. So he straightened up in his chair and steeled himself to receive a withering glare from Captain Dan.

The skipper was on his feet, about to leave for the pilot house. But he wasn't looking in the boy's direction. Instead, he was staring at Gold Brick, and Scott was puzzled by the look in his steel gray eyes. It seemed as though he was both angered and amused by the mining promoter's demonstration.

The arguments about panning gold went on. Scott and Jack were very hungry, so they ate busily as they listened. They were ready to leave the table while the others were still talking over their mugs of coffee. Scott would have liked to hear how the discussion ended, but when Jack signaled toward the door, he got up and followed him.

"It has stopped raining, believe it or not," Jack announced after a glance through the porthole of their cabin. "Get your jacket and we'll go up on deck."

"Gee whiz, Jack—I don't know—I want to keep away from the pilot house. First, I whistled; then I talked you into a hike and made us late getting back on board; then I acted like a kid and nearly upset the catsup. Seems as though I get in wrong every time I see the captain."

Jack's eyes twinkled. "Forget it—you worry too much. A while ago I could tell you were worrying about what to say when the fellows asked what happened on our expedition ashore. Well, nobody mentioned it—did they?"

So the two friends found a place on the upper deck where

they could stretch out with their backs against the fire-bucket rack. Here they were aft of the pilot house and out of the captain's sight. There was a strip of blue sky overhead and a mountain of black rock rose steeply—perhaps a mile back from the river's edge.

Gee-gee appeared at the head of the companionway and strutted over to join the boys.

"Reckon those fellers can get along without me, now the discussion is well under way." The wrangler seemed pleased with himself.

Scott grinned at him. "I notice you weren't saying much, but it sure started the ball rolling when you mentioned centrifugal force."

Gee-gee chuckled. "Always like to hear folks engaged in intelligent conversation. That was quite a demonstration Schnider put on, but a pan full o' gravel would be a mite heavier to handle than that soup plate."

"He seems to be a pretty smooth customer, if you ask me," Jack remarked. "But the others weren't letting him get away with anything, were they? They're surveyors, aren't they?"

"That's right—there's one or two survey parties come in every summer. Right smart bunch of fellows, they are, and they're doin' good work, fillin' in the blank spots on the maps. 'Tain't their fault the government has been sendin' them on a wild goose chase for the last couple o' years."

"What sort of a wild goose chase?" Scott noticed that Gee-gee's beard seemed to point outward as a sort of a warning signal when he was annoyed.

"All this foolishness about findin' a route for a highway into the Yukon and Alaska. That's what kind of a wild goose chase," the wrangler boomed. "Governments are always looking for ways to spend money, I 'spose. Wait until you see the Cassiar. Nice open jack pine and spruce country, good grazin' never too far away when you want to make camp. You don't need highways in a country where you can take a pack-string anywhere you want to go."

The boat altered course to follow a sharp bend in the channel and a biting chill from the mountains swept across the deck. Scott got up and paced back and forth to keep warm, and the others soon joined him. Off the port bow, he could see a vast sheet of ice spread over the mountainside—snow white where it emerged from the clouds to twist between the black pinnacles of rock, translucent blue where it fanned out at the water's edge.

"That's the Great Glacier." Gee-gee thrust his hands into the pockets of his blue jeans, and pulled his slouch hat to one side to shelter his face from the icy breeze. "Quite a chunk o' ice—'bout three miles across where she hits the river. Accordin' to the Indians, she used to stretch clear across the valley and the river ran under the ice. Just one o' their old fairy tales, I reckon."

Scott didn't answer, but he thought the Indian legend must be founded on fact. It was hard to imagine a great icecap covering this vast northern land, but he had read enough to know that, many thousands of years ago, it must have been so. Harder still to imagine the great upheavals, back in the beginning of time, which had thrust those jagged mountain peaks up into the clouds.

"Tomorrow mornin' we'll be pickin' up old Benjamin Arnett—'Beaver,' everybody calls him. Has one o' the best trap lines on the river. He's not hankerin' for any highway. Highways don't help in a fur country," Gee-gee rumbled on.

In spite of the roaring engines, which made the decks tremble under their feet, it seemed to Scott that it was taking the *Chutine* an endless time to crawl past the foot of the glacier.

"Yes sir!" Gee-gee's beard was bristling again. "Furs and big game trophies—that's about all there is in the Cassiar. These government fellows outside talk about highways openin' up the country. 'Vast mineral wealth,' they say. You can take that out in a buckskin poke. Like I've just done—cashed in two ounces of gold dust so I could get a fillin' put in my tooth. And that fillin' must weigh less than a pennyweight."

Jack murmured, "Well, I don't know anything about it, but I suppose the idea is that a lot of other things besides gold could be mined if there were a cheap way to get them to a market. I mean . . . well . . . things like iron ore and coal might . . ."

"Such as that there?" Gee-gee snorted and waved toward the mountains. "Just millions of tons of plain rock—no good to anyone."

Scott didn't argue with the old man, but somehow he knew there must be something more than just "plain rock" in the mountains. The placer gold buried in the gravel of the streams must have, long ago, been carried down from some rich vein of ore—the Mother Lode. Of course he had years of study ahead of him before he could understand about it. But, just the same, if he ever had the chance to go into the mountains at the source of Osprey Creek, he had made up his mind to keep his eyes open.

Would he recognize the Mother Lode if he did find it? Could he identify his rock samples if he ever saw them again? His thoughts swung back quickly to a more immediate problem. There was something strangely disturbing in the realization that someone had stolen those samples from his duffel bag—even if the culprit had been no more than a casual sneak thief.

Scott tried to put the memory out of his mind and concentrate on the new collection he was going to make. He turned to Jack.

"Just two more days on the river, and then I'll be picking up some samples of that plain rock."

Gee-gee paid no attention. He was too busy growling about the foolishness of people who wanted to build roads into the north country.

3

STEAMBOAT BEND

It was ten o'clock before twilight closed in on the valley, and the *Chutine* was snugged down for the short nothern night. Two deck hands scrambled over a freshly washed gravel beach to make her lines fast to the spruce trees towering above the bank.

Standing on the fore deck, Scott sniffed the sharp tang of the evergreens and thought how much fresher it was than the dankness of the jungle at the Boundary. That walk in the woods seemed almost like a dream now. It had been a long day.

Now that they had left the glaciers behind, the valley had widened out, and timber-covered slopes rose gently from the other side of the river. The peaks of the mountains were bundled in clouds which glowed like burnished gold. Scott looked up at them. Sort of sunset and sunrise rolled into one, he thought drowsily.

"Watch those lines tonight—the water's dropping fast." The captain was giving final instructions to the hand on night watch duty.

Minutes later, curled up under the blankets in his upper berth, Scott thought of that golden light in the late evening sky. It was proof that they were heading northward.

Two more days on the river . . . three days over the portage . . .

There was no sound now except the soft swish and gurgle of the river lapping against the hull, and Scott quickly dropped into a sound sleep.

At three o'clock—Scott could tell the time by holding his watch up in the gray dawn light filtering through the porthole—he was awakened by a shattering series of explosions as the engines came to life. He heard a muffled voice shouting an order—footsteps on the deck above him—then the clang of the engine room gong and the engines settled down to their steady throb.

Scott thought of Captain Dan up in the pilot house. His eyes, even at this early hour, would have to be alert to every swirl and ripple that might tell of hidden danger in the river. On him alone rested the responsibility for the safe delivery of the cargo—for the very lives of the passengers resting peacefully below.

Scott slipped off to sleep again, thinking that it was no wonder the captain never seemed to smile. The next time he awoke, the cook's hand bell was ringing for breakfast.

As the two boys came away from the breakfast table, Jack let out a notch in his belt. "You know, I think we're both eating too much."

Scott grinned. "You may have something there. Things aren't dished up so fancy as they were on the steamer, but there's so much good grub right there in front of you, it's hard to resist."

To counteract the effect of the tall stacks of flapjacks they had eaten, they went on deck and walked briskly back and forth. Scott took good care to see that they turned at the end of each lap before they came into view from the pilot house.

After their breakfast seemed well shaken down, the pair stopped at the stern railing and watched the maelstrom of foam boiling up from the wake.

Jack exclaimed, "Lots of power there! Did you realize this was a twin screw job?"

"No kidding?"

"Sure! Come down and have a look at the engine room. The propellers are in tunnels under the hull and they can hoist them up when they hit shallow water." Jack led the way to introduce Scott to the Chief.

A few minutes later, Scott stood looking at the wake with fresh enthusiasm. "Golly! The Chief says he doesn't open her up until we come to the canyons—the engines are just at half-throttle now."

"Yes, sir!" Jack beamed. "The little *Chutine* is specially built for the job. With 'full ahead' on one engine and 'full astern' on the other, I'll bet she could turn on a dime. At first I thought she was just a scow . . ." Jack's eulogy of the *Chutine* was interrupted by the lunch bell.

Half an hour later the two boys were back on deck.

"I still say we're eating too much," Jack remarked, and they started to pace vigorously back and forth.

Suddenly Scott pointed to an open gap on the timber-covered bank. "Look—there's a cabin. This must be where we're going to pick up that trapper, the one they call Beaver." He felt a peculiar thrill. This was the first sign of human habitation they had seen since they left the Boundary.

The boys went down on the fore deck as the *Chutine* approached the foot of the pathway that led down the bank. Scott could see Beaver at the top of the path now. He appeared too small for the enormous curved pipe clamped in his teeth, and he seemed dwarfed by the bulging pack sack and two canvas bundles stacked beside him.

He didn't look as if he weighed as much as Scott, the boy thought. But the dog beside him could really be called a giant. It was a sandy, reddish dog with wide, floppy ears and a long, scrawny tail. Its head was almost level with Beaver's shoulders.

That wasn't a northern Husky, Scott decided. He couldn't think of any breed it did resemble—nevertheless the creature held up his head as proudly as any thoroughbred as he gazed at his master.

Beaver clutched the bowl of his pipe and pointed the stem toward the pilot house. "How d'you do, Captain. Well—I told you I'd be going with you this trip. Guess you've known me long enough to know I wouldn't go back on my word. I always say, if a feller is going to get on in this world . . ."

"All right! All right!" The skipper barked. "Get your dunnage on board and we'll shove off."

Beaver came down to the landing and deposited his

pack sack on the fore deck. "How d'you do—how d'you do." He nodded to Jack and Scott. "Say, do you young fellers mind giving me a hand with that bale of beaver skins up there?"

The two boys were off up the bank before the trapper had a chance to say another word. But when they got within a couple of yards of the two bales of fur, the dog crouched before them with his teeth bared. The hair on the back of his neck bristled a warning to keep away.

Scott remembered the rule—never let a dog know you're afraid of him. But this seemed to be an unusual sort of a dog.

"Here—here—g-o-o-d boy!" Jack coaxed. But he was answered with a deep-throated growl.

Scott felt that the hair on the back of his own neck was standing up. Glancing back, he saw Beaver, who had stopped for a moment to talk to one of the crew, running up behind them.

"Dinty! Cut that out, you old fool. That's better." Beaver fondled one of the big flop ears, and with his other hand pointed the stem of his pipe at Jack.

"Shucks—I'm sorry. I should have introduced you to Dinty. I guess he gets a little queer, what with being down here on the trap line all winter and never seeing anyone but me."

"What's your name, young fellow? . . . Jack? . . . That's fine. Dinty, shake hands with Jack."

Jack looked very pleased with himself as he held the big paw in his hand, and Dinty seemed in no hurry to withdraw it.

"And your name? . . . Scott—eh? All right, Dinty, this is Scott."

Placid, amber-colored eyes turned to look at Scott, but the boy didn't get time to shake hands with Dinty. The captain was shouting, demanding to know what in blazes was holding things up.

Scott led a scramble into the freight deck. There it seemed cool and peaceful, out of range of the skipper's blistering words.

Minutes later the *Chutine* was rumbling on upstream. The three of them were seated comfortably on Beaver's packs, and Dinty was stretched out with his chin across Jack's feet.

"Well, sir," old Beaver said, "I suppose you expected a trapper to be a regular wild man from the mountains, dressed in a buckskin shirt instead of a blue serge suit like mine. But you might figure me as just sort of a rancher, with my livestock out to pasture, scattered over twenty miles or so of bush country.

"Take this year, for instance. I heard that mink prices would be down, so I said to myself, 'Me and Dinty will just go after the marten and beaver.' Then, when there weren't as many marten around as I'd figured on, I made up for it by trapping more beaver. Well—I made it— enough to pay for my outfit, with a little left over.

" 'Course I didn't clean out all the beaver lodges by any means. That would have been like a farmer selling all his cows and calves to the butcher."

Scott noticed that Jack seemed to be taking in every word, but he found his own thoughts wandering. He wasn't particularly interested in furs. He gazed enviously at Jack with the dog sprawled at his feet.

"Scratch his ear, Scott, so's he'll get to know you." Beaver paused to suck at his pipe, which had gone out long ago.

Dinty allowed his ear to be scratched. But rather grudgingly, Scott thought, because the dog's eyes shifted slowly from Beaver to Jack without glancing at him.

" 'Course he's a one-man dog." Beaver tried to sound apologetic.

"A one-man dog!" Scott echoed. "I've always wanted a dog of my own, and that's the kind I'm going to pick out some day."

"That kind of a dog picks you out." Beaver kept his eyes fixed on Dinty. "Perhaps, though, we'll see you coming out this fall with one of those little Tahltan Bear Dogs. Hard to say though—there aren't many good ones left. The Tahltan Indians used them for hunting long before the white man came to this country, and they're the smartest little critters on four legs—don't let anybody try to tell you anything different. If one of those dogs ever took up with you, you'd sure be lucky."

Late in the afternoon, the two boys and Beaver stood on the upper deck, with the sheer rock walls of the canyon rising less than a hundred feet away on either side of them. The *Chutine* seemed almost motionless for minutes at a time as she met the full force of the river compressed into this narrow gorge. Then, slowly, she crept over to an eddy close under the canyon wall and started to forge ahead.

Scott supposed those brownish-gray rock walls were granite. How many thousands of years had it taken the river to cut a channel through the solid rock? It sort of took his breath away to think about it!

Time seemed to stand still as the *Chutine* shivered in the shadow of the rock walls. Scott hadn't looked at his watch, but he estimated it was about twenty minutes before the river widened out and tree-lined banks appeared on both sides of them.

"A good stage of water for bucking the canyon." Beaver jabbed his pipe-stem at Scott. "If the river had been up like it was a couple of weeks ago, we might have had to tie up for a day or two."

He spoke casually—an extra day or so tied up along the river would have meant little to the trapper. But Scott's lower lip stuck out as he realized what the extra delay would have meant to him—another two days added to his trip into Osprey Creek!

"We should be past Steamboat Bend before dark," Beaver remarked. "We'll be in Telegraph Creek before noon tomorrow."

It seemed to Scott that the mountains and woods, bathed in golden sunlight, were welcoming him as the boat emerged from the shadow of the rugged Coast Range. A brisk wind was blowing from astern, making little dust devils skip across a gravel bar in midstream. Even the warm, dry air felt friendly now, it seemed to be helping the boat along.

Beaver pointed his pipe at the dust devils. "That's the old Stikine wind ablowing. All summer she whoops upstream like that."

Well—the wind couldn't whip a narrow river into dangerous waves, so that was nothing to worry about. Scott's spirits were high when he went below for dinner with Beaver and Jack.

As they took their places at the table, Gold Brick was talking rapidly in a low voice to Gee-gee. When he noticed Scott, he broke off abruptly, in the middle of a sentence, but not before the boy had caught a few of his words. "He'll find out he can't do it alone. . . . A mine like that needs a bunch of men with money behind it . . . or a syndicate. . . . Too big a risk for one man. . . ."

It was at this point that Gold Brick stopped and uttered the ever-familiar greeting: "Hi, Scotty!"

"Hi!" Scott grunted and sat down. The back of his neck was prickling. A strange apprehension seized and nearly choked him. *A mine like that.* He still heard Gold Brick's voice and remembered his startled glance when he had looked up at him. Did Gee-gee agree with what Gold Brick had been saying? Scott glanced at the old man but found no answer in his poker face.

All Scott's doubts and worries crowded back into his mind. Of course they must have been talking about his father's mine. He recalled the voices in the freight deck at the Boundary. "All the gold they ship out won't weigh much." And his father had said the mine *had* to pay this year—or else!

Scott's gaze shifted from Gee-gee's expressionless face. He caught Jack's eyes smiling at him across the table. As unaccountably as it had come, his uneasiness left him.

And the meat course was roast pork that had been in the oven just the right length of time to surround it with crisp "cracklings." There was applesauce to go with it and there were vegetables crowned with rich brown gravy. The food on the *Chutine* was something to write home about. Just eating seemed to lift Scott's spirits again. No doubt Jack was right—perhaps he did worry too much.

When they were up on deck once more, Scott and Jack made a game of guessing which channel the skipper was going to take. The river had widened out again and was dotted with tree-covered islands, the channels between them were often tortuous and swift. Sometimes both the boys guessed wrong and they marveled as the captain found a gap between two islands, a gap which to them was invisible until the *Chutine* was almost into it.

They entered a second canyon and the deck trembled as they roared through it. But the channel was not so narrow, nor the water so swift, as it had been in the first canyon.

"Kloochman Canyon—we're making good time," said Beaver, who had joined the boys with Gee-gee.

"Kloochman—that's the Chinook word for woman," the wrangler boomed. "Guess they called this Kloochman Canyon 'cause even a woman could run it in a dugout canoe."

As he spoke, they could see more islands ahead. The Kloochman was gentle compared to the first canyon. Jack pushed back his curly hair, which had blown down over his forehead, and shaded his eyes from the low slanting sun.

"I'll say the channel to the left of that island ahead."

Scott shrugged his shoulders and grinned. "I'll have to take the only other guess then—to the right."

Beaver nudged Gee-gee with his pipe. "Captain Dan'll fool these young fellers this time. Shoal water in both those channels now—we'll have to go around by Steamboat Bend. Kind of a tricky turn with this wind blowing. Bad name the Bend has."

"Pshaw!" Gee-gee roared. "I know it's called Steamboat Bend because one of the old stern-wheelers piled up there. But it wouldn't have happened to a boat with twin screws—though with all this top-hamper, she's bound to be blown around a bit by these winds."

The bow swung steadily to the right until the boat was heading at right angles to the channel they had been following. Scott realized how wrong both his guess and Jack's had been.

The boat moved slowly. Scott felt the wind on his right cheek, and he noticed the long shadow of the ensign staff wavering across the deck. There was something odd about that shadow—it hadn't been there before.

Then it dawned on him that, with the sun in the northwest, the shadow meant the boat had swung almost completely around. Looking toward the bow, he saw that she was headed straight for the bank, until, miraculously it seemed, a channel opened up to his left.

He heard the engine room gong clang and felt the superstructure quiver as the Chief opened the throttle. Dark and smooth, the river slid past the bank directly ahead. And then the bow swung back and pointed toward the gap, and on his left he could see silvery ripples dancing over the shallows.

Scott was beginning to understand. The main channel of the river made a hairpin turn around the point of an island here—and the deep water was close to the east bank. They were starting to swing back toward the sun now—another two hundred yards and the *Chutine* would be safely around Steamboat Bend. A long, straight stretch of water was opening up ahead, when a violent gust of wind swung her off course.

Gongs clanged furiously in the engine room. The engines snarled and the bow wheeled into the teeth of the wind. Then from somewhere down below came a muffled thud. Scott felt as though somebody had suddenly struck the deck beneath him with a mallet. The shock seemed to jar his teeth and bounce his heart into his throat. Something had happened to the boat that could "turn on a dime"!

"Snag!" Gee-gee's bellow boomed through the echo of the noises below.

For a few seconds a strange, uneven vibration shuddered through the framework of the deckhouse, and then the port engine stopped. Scott stood rooted to the deck and watched the *Chutine* veer off to port, caught in the grip of the wind and the eddies of the backwater that curled around the point. With only one engine left, it was a losing struggle. She slipped suddenly from the slanting sunlight into the shadow of a wooded island and crunched hard aground on the gravel.

Jack and Beaver, who had gone below to investigate, came back on deck.

"They think it must have been a sunken log," Jack announced. "Got tangled up in the port tunnel—sprung a leak in it and damaged the propeller."

Beaver sucked at his gurgling pipe. "The cap'n put her ashore in the best spot he could pick. The way the water's going down, the port screw will be high and dry by morning. Everybody who can handle an ax will be working all night to cut down trees to make skids so we can warp her off in the morning. But, shucks—there won't be much to it, though Cap'n Dan'll take it hard. 'Twasn't his fault. We won't blame him and he should know that. It was plain bad luck—that's all it was."

Bad luck! Scott felt a gnawing sensation in the pit of his stomach. What was it Captain Dan had called him? "Confounded little Jonah!" Scott knew that, to a sailor, a Jonah was a person who brought misfortune to a ship. Would the skipper blame him, then, for their present predicament? Would he think it was all because Scott had whistled in the pilothouse? With a feeling that he was terribly in the way, he watched the crew and the surveyors going ashore and saw Captain Dan stalk up and point to Gee-gee, Beaver and Jack.

"You'll find axes down below."

Scott waited anxiously for the skipper to speak to him. But the captain just stood staring at the far bank of the river. Better to speak now, before his courage oozed away.

Scott had a slightly jutting chin, and he tried to make it stand out like Gee-gee's beard as he looked the captain straight in the eye.

"Is there any way I could lend a hand, Captain?"

The captain turned his head and his steely eyes looked into Scott's. "Why . . . yes . . . I'll give you something to do."

A glow of satisfaction kindled inside Scott, but it was quickly extinguished by the skipper's next words.

"Keep out of our way for a while. Go and turn in and I'll . . ."

"Hi! Captain!" The shout sent the skipper hurrying to the fore deck.

The boy stood for a few minutes on the deserted upper deck. There was no sign of the captain coming back. Dejectedly, Scott hunched his shoulders as he walked aft and shuffled down the companionway.

4

CAPTAIN DAN'S MESSAGE

"WAKE up, Lad! You and I have a job to do."

Scott twisted in his bunk and pushed aside the hand that was shaking his shoulder.

"Wha's matter?" There was suppressed annoyance in his voice, for he had been sleeping very soundly. Then he remembered bitterly the captain ordering him to turn in while everyone else was working. His ears seemed to be ringing still with the sound of axes biting into green timber ashore, and the clank of metal in the engine room. Those were the sounds he had been hearing as he tossed and turned before he finally dropped off to sleep.

It seemed as if that had been only a few minutes ago. Propping himself up on his elbow, he rubbed the sleep out of his eyes and recognized Beaver standing in the faint pre-dawn light filtering through the porthole. The trapper's chin was covered with a thin stubble of gray beard—his cheeks weren't so brown and shiny as they had been when he came on board.

"A job! What kind of a job?" Scott's voice sounded

uncertain and sceptical. When the captain ordered him to his cabin, he hadn't sounded as if there was any task for Scott that would amount to anything.

"A mighty important job. They're taking us across the river in the skiff. We're to hook a couple of lines over tree stumps and stand by for the signal to let them go. If we can do it right on the dot, the boat will make the turn. . . . If we don't . . . well . . ." Beaver waved his hand in a half-circle.

"Better put on some warm clothes—it's a bit nippy on the river before the sun comes up. If you hurry, there'll be time for a cup of coffee before we get going." The old man clamped his pipe in his teeth and seemed to crawl out through the door.

The boy was aware for the first time that the deck had a slight list; apparently the boat had settled to starboard as the water dropped. But the slant of the deck was not steep enough to make walking difficult.

Scott splashed cold water on his face and pulled on his clothes. He wasn't very clear about what lay ahead of him. Letting go a line didn't sound like much of a job; but at least it would be better than standing around, watching the others work.

In the dining saloon, sleepy-eyed men were crowded around the table, drinking coffee. Scott couldn't help noticing that Beaver looked very old—and very frail.

"Boy! Am I *tired?*" Jack spread out his hands—he had a blister on the right palm. Somehow Scott felt a little envious of that blister.

"Everything is under control now," Jack went on.

"We've got the timbers in place under the hull to slide her off. The Chief and his gang patched the hole in the tunnel. And the water went down far enough so they could get at the propeller—wasn't as bad as it might have been. The prop is bronze, it seems, and they were able to hammer the blades back into shape without even taking it off the shaft."

Scott gulped down a cup of scalding coffee, then followed Beaver out to the foredeck and down onto the gravel bar. There was a faint salmon-pink glow overhead. The air was cool and fresh and faintly perfumed by the pitch from the freshly hewn timbers.

The sound of the captain's voice behind him startled Scott.

"We'll have to get started before the wind gets up." Scott turned around. It was the captain's voice, but it didn't sound harsh and angry—just matter of fact, almost gentle. The skipper went on. "We'll pull ourselves off by our bootstraps, a bowline and a stern line hooked over the stumps of two trees the men have felled on the other bank. We have a power capstan on the foredeck to haul on the bowline, but we'll have to use a block and tackle to manhandle the stern line. We'll need all the strong backs for that job, and we'll have to count on you two being on your toes."

The captain's tone was brisk and serious.

"You'll look after the stern line, Scott. As soon as we get the stern swung off, I'll give you a blast on the whistle and you'll slip the bight off the stump. Beaver will be on the bowline—we won't be able to give him enough slack to let it go until we're nearly in midstream."

Two deck hands were already in the flat-bottomed skiff, one making fast the bight of a wire cable to a midship thwart, the other standing by the outboard motor. Just as Beaver was climbing into the boat Dinty came loping over the gravel. The deck hands shouted at him to keep back. But Beaver protested, "He won't be a mite of trouble, Cap'n; he's used to boats."

"Looks as if he is all right," the captain grunted, for Dinty had already scrambled into the skiff and was flattened out on the floor boards.

Scott, crouched in the bow, felt the skipper squeeze his shoulder and heard him mutter, "Good luck—don't forget —those lines have to be clear as soon as you get the signals, or I'll never be able to swing her in time to clear the bend."

Captain Dan pushed the bow clear of the beach. The man at the stern whipped back the starting cord and the kicker machine-gunned into life. Scott felt the cold spray in his face as the square bow slapped into the swells. Soon he could see that the far bank was a sheer wall of clay and gravel, rising ten or fifteen feet above the river. The current boiled and surged along the bank. Trees on the slope were half toppling over, their roots undermined during the spring flood.

Slowly, with bow angling upstream, the boat slid in closer to the bank. Scott was wondering how they were ever going to land without being dashed against the bank, when the skiff nosed into the mouth of a creek and came to rest against a small gravel bar which sheltered them from the swirling waters of the river.

The man at the stern stopped the engine, and all aboard jumped ashore and hauled the boat out. Dinty had already started up a rough trail. The men followed him, dragging the wire cable with them. The bight of the cable they placed over the stump of a fresh-felled tree at the top of the bank. The man who had been running the kicker pointed out to Scott a newly blazed trail, leading downstream. "There's your trail—you can't miss it—about a hundred and fifty yards down there you'll come to a fresh stump," he explained. "Just stand by, and we'll be along to toss you a heaving line. One thing to remember—don't get too close to the edge. The high water has undercut the bank and she'd be liable to cave in on you."

Scott turned down the trail. It was remarkably easy to follow. There was a soft cushion of pine needles underfoot, and even though the trail was still shaded from the morning sun, the woods seemed dry and smelled fresh and clean.

As Scott waited for the skiff to come, he looked across the river to where the rays of the sun lit up the sparkling white deckhouse of the *Chutine*. He thought he could make out Jack, and Gee-gee, and Gold Brick in the group at the stern. For a moment he felt lonely and far away from them. He thought of Beaver, as he had left him, with Dinty watching his every move. You never would feel lonely if you had a dog like that.

But Scott didn't have long to think about the old trapper and his dog, because the skiff was coming back now. It drew in under the bank. Soon it was so close that he couldn't see it. He could tell it was there only by the *bur-r-r-r* of the kicker. And then the heaving-line landed with a thud on the pine needles. He hauled it in, hand over hand, until the end of the cable appeared, and he slipped the loop over the stump.

How about the heaving-line? Nobody had said anything about that. He considered for a moment and decided it would be rather sloppy to leave it attached to the cable. So he loosened the clove hitch from the wire, coiled up the light line, and slung it across his shoulder.

Quickly now the wire cable straightened out and cut a groove in the soft earth at the edge of the bank. The stump creaked, and Scott could imagine the gang on the *Chutine* hauling on the block and tackle. Looking across the river, he could see the line tauten and lift clear of the water for almost its entire length, and the *Chutine* was afloat! The crackle of her exhaust echoing across the valley made her seem alive again. The strain on the cable eased.

No signal yet—but Scott moved expectantly closer to the stump. He had begun to wonder if the noise of the exhaust could have drowned out the whistle, when the staccato hoot took his breath away. The cable lay limp along the ground beside him now. He merely pulled the bight off the stump, and as he let go of it, it wriggled swiftly over the bank like a snake.

Nothing to this, he thought as he started back toward Beaver. Just as he caught sight of the old trapper, he heard the hoot of the second signal. Beaver tugged at the bight of the cable, but there seemed to be something wrong. He couldn't get it free from the stump!

A series of blasts from the whistle in quick succession!

What was the trouble? Scott started to run; the trail led him through a grove of trees which cut off his view. When he emerged, there was the stump with the cable still attached, fresh broken earth where it disappeared over the bank—but no sign of Beaver and Dinty.

Scott put all his strength into sprinting across the few yards that separated him from the stump. There had apparently been a terrific strain on the bowline, for the wire had cut deep into the green wood. But it was slack now, and Scott worked it back and forth a couple of times to pull it out of the groove it had cut and lift it clear.

Somewhere below him, he could hear Dinty barking, and suddenly it dawned on him what had happened. Beaver had gone too close to the edge and the bank had caved in.

Scott still had the bight of the cable in his hands. He thought of the swirling eddies sucking at the river's edge. "Beaver! Beaver!" he shouted at the top of his lungs. "Are you all right?"

"Never mind about me, Scott. Get that line clear and mind you keep back from the edge. By Jimminy! Forty years trapping along the river, and now I get myself into a crazy fool jackpot like this." Relief brought a half-smile to Scott's lips. Beaver was safe for the moment—safe and sound but hopping mad!

Scott moved upstream a few yards before he let go of the line. He had to be sure it would fall clear of the old man.

His thoughts were racing as the cable slithered out of sight. He could picture Beaver clinging desperately to the crumbling clay as the river steadily undermined his foot-hold. He must act, and act quickly, to save Beaver. But how? The heaving-line—it was still across his shoulder! He shrugged off the rope and forced his hands to move steadily as he bent a bowline on one end. He slipped the bight over the stump and, reaching far back with perfect rhythm, he heaved the coil over the bank.

The line jerked tight. There was the sound of gravel sliding down the bank beyond his sight. And then, after a breathless minute, Beaver's gray head appeared and Dinty's huge forepaws clawed at the crumbling edge of the bank. Beaver had one hand on the line, the other clutched the dog's collar.

Scott heard the quickening snarl of the *Chutine*'s engines and caught a glimpse of her square stern as she roared up the swift, straight stretch of water beyond Steamboat Bend. Dinty shook himself and lay down beside the stump. Beaver, dripping wet from the waist down, his clothes smeared with sand and clay, came toward Scott like an indignant bantam rooster.

"Bight o' the line jammed in the stump . . . couldn't get her loose . . . just went over to heave on the cable to get some slack. Then all of a sudden . . . down I went like an otter down his slide. Next thing I knew I was up to my middle in the river, with Dinty holding me by the scruff of the neck."

Scott's face was solemn as he coiled up the heaving-line. The thought of the treacherous whirlpools that Beaver had so narrowly escaped sent a cold chill up his spine.

"I'll get a fire going so you can dry out," he suggested.

"Shucks, no need for that. As soon as the boat gets past the swift water, they'll be sending the skiff back for us. I'm fine and dandy now. Right smart of you to have had that heaving line handy, though. Don't know if Dinty and I could have held out much longer."

Beaver fished in his pocket and produced his pipe. He seemed to be able to express himself better when he had it in his hand.

"You know, Scott, I 'spose that old river is going to get me some day. I guess it's only right that it should. Long time now I've been making a living off this river."

Scott could think of nothing to say. He was silent while they walked down to the gravel bar to wait for the skiff. As they suddenly stepped out into the sunshine, he stooped to examine a greenish pebble. It felt warm in his hand.

"Oh, boy! That sun feels good."

" 'Course it does. You're in the Cassiar now." Beaver looked up at the clear sky. "All the clouds are behind, on the other side of the mountains. She's going to be a fine day, and we'll only be a few hours late getting in. Everything will be hunky-dory now."

A few minutes later, sitting in the bow of the skiff, Scott could think of no better word than "hunky-dory" to describe his feelings. The rays of the morning sun in the valley ahead had turned the somber tones of the terraced mountainsides to bright green. The jagged peaks of the Coast Range were behind them, they were safely through the Canyon and around Steamboat Bend. He was made comfortably drowsy by the drone of the kicker.

Certainly everything seemed to be hunky-dory now.

As Scott climbed onto the *Chutine*'s fore deck, Jack was there to greet him. Jack's eyes were red from lack of sleep, but a grin flickered across his face. . . . "Some fun, huh?"

One of the surveyors greeted Scott with, "Hi there!" and another asked, "Well, how's she going?"

Gold Brick's expensive looking clothes were rumpled and his mouth seemed to sag, as though he were almost too tired to move his thick lips as he spoke.

"*We* have all been working, Scotty. How did you manage to wangle such a soft job?"

The words startled Scott, but some instinct made him answer lightly. "Oh! Brains . . . know-how . . . just a little extra something you fellows didn't have, I guess."

Gee-gee slapped his thigh and whooped. "By crikey! You're doin' all right, Scott—that's tellin' him."

A ripple of friendly laughter echoed Gee-gee's guffaw, and only now did Scott realize that most of the passengers, and several of the crew, were gathered on the deck. Scott laughed from deep down inside himself. He didn't mind whether they were laughing at him or with him; he could take all the kidding they wanted to fire at him. He was one of the gang now.

The engines started up, the boat swung out from the bank, and once more the *Chutine* was rumbling upstream. From inside came the tinkle of the breakfast bell and everybody moved toward the dining saloon.

"This is what we've been waiting for." Jack pretended to be taking up a notch in his belt. "I think I'll just have a light breakfast this morning; there'll be no walk on deck afterwards. I'm going to hit the sack and catch up on my shut-eye."

"Scott!" the captain shouted down from the pilothouse. "Come up here for a minute."

"Don't look so worried—he's not going to keel-haul you." Jack nudged his friend in the ribs and disappeared aft.

Easy enough for Jack to make a crack like that, Scott thought, as he climbed the companion ladder. Jack wasn't the one who had to face the captain. But what was Scott supposed to do? Apologize for whistling in the pilot house? Did the skipper really hold him responsible for the bad luck at Steamboat Bend?

Scott squared his shoulders and thrust out his lower lip as he reached the pilot house. But there seemed to be a smile in the skipper's eyes.

"Won't keep you long—I know you need your breakfast and some sleep." Scott marveled at the gentleness in Captain Dan's voice.

"I was watching you through the field glasses. No one else on board could see what was happening when Beaver slid down the bank. Lucky for him you kept your head and went at the job in a proper, shipshape way."

The captain turned for a moment and Scott looked into steel-gray eyes—not stern and cold, but warm and friendly. Everything really was hunky-dory now.

There was a song of joy in his heart. But he kept it inside him and merely murmured, "There . . . wasn't much to it."

"No?" The skipper was watching the river now. "What kind of a knot did you tie on the end of that heaving-line?"

"A bowline."

"*H-m-m,* didn't take you long. Where did you learn that?"

"In the Scouts."

"Mighty good training, from what I've seen. What else do they teach you?"

"Oh, all sorts of things." Odd—Scott thought. There were so many things he had learned in the Scouts, but it seemed hard to decide which were the most important ones. . . . "Swimming, hiking, camping out, first aid . . . things like that."

"I'll bet it will all come in handy to you before the summer's over." The skipper remained silent for a long minute, studying the river. Behind him, Scott squirmed impatiently, for he was very hungry and sleepy. The captain's approval of what he had done seemed to have freed his mind from all doubts and worries. He felt that he would like to turn in and sleep for the rest of the day.

Suddenly the skipper stepped back and stood close to him. "Your dad showed me the samples from his ground at Osprey Creek." He had lowered his voice, apparently so the man at the wheel couldn't hear him. "It's been tough going for him for the last two seasons, but I'm sure he'll be into rich pay dirt this summer. Wouldn't like to see him get discouraged and sell out to some tinhorn outfit. I want you to give him this message from me."

Scott fumbled in his shirt pocket for his notebook, but the captain shook his head. "Best not to write it down

—and don't mention it to anyone—it's just one of my hunches. Tell him to remember the Jack o' Diamonds Claim on Magpie Creek."

Scott murmured, "Jack o' Diamonds on Magpie."

Captain Dan cut in, "Your father will have to be on his toes. Are you sure you have it straight?"

"Remember the Jack o' Diamonds Claim on Magpie Creek," Scott repeated in a whisper.

The skipper nodded. "You've got it! Better go below and get your breakfast now."

For a moment Scott thought of telling about the loss of his rock samples, but that didn't seem to matter so much now. There had been a note of concern in the captain's voice that made him sense an urgent warning in the cryptic message.

Scott stepped on deck into the sunshine. In spite of a vague worry that his father might not get the message in time, he felt like singing. Captain Dan had confidence in him! Osprey Creek was getting closer. It could only be a few more days before he gave his father the captain's message.

5

GEE-GEE'S STRANGE BEHAVIOR

Scott stood at the fore railing and watched the buildings creeping into view on the terraced riverbank ahead.
The *Chutine* seemed to be taking forever to crawl up
this last mile of swift water. The pillared rock ramparts
towering above the bank were edged in flame from the
sunset, and twilight had fallen into the valley.

"Hum-ho!" Jack came from the companionway, rubbing his eyes. "You should have splashed cold water on
me to wake me up."

"You looked so peaceful, I didn't have the heart."

"I needed some shut-eye," Jack admitted. "Hope I
didn't miss anything, though. What's new?"

Scott hesitated. It would be fine to be free to tell Jack
about the message: *Remember the Jack o' Diamonds.*
But he had been warned not to tell anyone but his father.

Scott shrugged his shoulders. "Not much. You're just
in time—we'll be in soon. You can see the warehouses and
some of the cabins now."

"Looks as if it won't be long before I take off my coat

and get to work," Jack said. "But we don't seem to be making much time."

However, within half an hour, the *Chutine* sidled along-side the dock. The engines stopped and for several minutes there was no sound but the lapping and gurgling of the river. Scott looked up and decided that the entire popu-lation of the settlement must be standing on the bank, staring down at the new arrivals with critical eyes. He felt like a specimen under a microscope.

"Well, there she is." Gee-gee slapped him on the shoul-der. "Capital of the Cassiar. No trouble to pick out the folks who live here—they walk sort o' catty-wampus from climbing up and down the sidehills."

That seemed to break the spell. The deck hands started to carry the mail sacks ashore and people swarmed down the gangway from the dock. Jack headed below, calling, "See you later, Scott. I'll have to get up to the store and report for work."

A wide-shouldered, steel-gray giant, whose height was emphasized by a black felt hat with no crease in the crown, extended a huge paw. "Scott Haliburton, I take it."

Scott accepted the crushing handshake.

"I'm Tim Donovan," the big man explained. "I look after the freight for the Dease River. The cat got in yesterday—before I forget about it, here's a letter from your father."

Scott grasped the envelope eagerly and stuffed it into his pocket. His bag had been ready to go ashore hours ago, but he muttered something about having to finish packing and rushed back to his cabin. He had to read that letter right away, but he didn't want anyone else around when he opened it.

Inside the envelope was a note, written in pencil on a page torn from a pocket notebook. There was no mistaking his father's neat, flowing hand, but instinctively Scott knew that the message had been written in a great hurry. His brow wrinkled with worry as he read it:

Dear Son:

There should be a shipment of hydraulic pipe on the *Chutine* this trip. We need it in the worst way so we can set up another monitor to keep the tailings clear.

I want you to keep after the freighters and make sure that they bring this pipe in right away. You will have to be tactful, but at the same time be firm and show them you mean business. Hydraulic pipe makes an awkward, bulky load and they'll probably come up with all sorts of excuses for leaving it until another trip.

Am looking forward to seeing you—*and a load of pipe*—in a few days. If we don't get it, we'll have to shut down—just at the time we stand a good chance of making the mine pay.

The freighters are a happy-go-lucky bunch and I can't always count on them bringing in what I ask for in a hurry. So you're the only one I can depend on and I know you'll do your best.

Good luck, Son,
Dad

Tight-lipped, Scott stood up and thrust the letter back into his pocket. Sure he'd be tactful. He'd wait and see how things turned out, though—perhaps Tim would decide to load the pipe first, anyway. He slung his dunnage bag over his shoulder and started back.

Tim was talking to Gee-gee and Beaver when Scott came out on the fore deck. He set his bag down, saying, "I'll go back and get my bedroll."

Scott dodged around a pile of boxes and sacks which the deck hands had carried out from the freight deck. "Golly!" he said to himself. "From the looks of that square jaw, if I try to show Tim I mean business, he's liable to be pig-headed as all get out."

Scott could see the lengths of black iron pipe piled up like big cord-wood sticks in the shadows at the far end of the freight compartment. He hadn't realized there was so much of it. The bulk of it seemed to dwarf the rest of the cargo now. He brushed past one solitary length of pipe standing on end—a little taller than himself, it loomed in the half-light, like a solitary, mocking human figure.

When Scott arrived back on deck, Gold Brick was standing with one foot on a box, making some notes in a small book he was holding on his knee.

"If you're in that much of a rush, I can't help you," Gee-gee drawled. "My hosses are all booked up for ten days, at least. Try Hank Young, he'll probably let you have three or four of his and get hold of a wrangler for you."

"Okay." Gold Brick flipped the notebook shut and turned to Scott. "Pile your dunnage alongside mine there and I'll have it sent up in the truck to the hotel."

"You needn't bother—Scott's staying at my cabin." Tim's mouth opened and shut like a steel trap.

For a second or two Gold Brick stood with the corner of his mouth twitching; his eyes shifting from the dun-

nage bag to the freight compartment. Then he turned
and stepped briskly up the gangway. "All right—I'll be
seeing you around. I'll have to get busy now and rustle up
those horses."

Tim picked up Scott's bag as though it were a sack of
peanuts and said to Gee-gee and Beaver, "Come up to
the cabin and I'll brew you some coffee. They're putting
the freight in the warehouse tonight—I won't load the
wagons 'til tomorrow."

Tomorrow—Scott's lower lip stuck out at the sound of
the word. But what could he say? What could he do?

They climbed the steep steps to the first terrace. Scott
stepped along impatiently, with short, uneven strides. He
wasn't used to strolling along at the leisurely pace of the
three men.

Five minutes later they came to Tim's log cabin, on the
bank of the mountain stream which gurgled through the
center of the settlement. The twilight was deeper here
beneath a clump of alders. The air was cool beside the
running water and it was aromatic with the fragrance of
a lone Balm of Gilead tree which towered behind the
cabin.

Tim pushed open the unlocked door and lifted the lid
of the stove, where pine shavings awaited the touch of
a match. As the kindling started to crackle and Tim slid
the coffeepot over the fire, Scott could conceal his
impatience no longer.

"What time will the cat-train be leaving tomorrow?"

Tim selected a stick from the wood box and poked it
into the stove. "It'll take all morning to load up—mebbe

longer. Nothing to be gained by pulling out tomorrow."

A frown crinkled between Scott's eyebrows. "Wouldn't it be a good idea to start as soon as the wagons are loaded?"

Gee-gee rumbled, "Calm down, Scott—that would just mean three nights on the trail instead of two. The way things stand, that mix-up at Steamboat Bend has put another day on your trip, whichever way you figure it out."

"Doesn't pay to be in too much of a hurry." Beaver was cramming tobacco into his pipe. It seemed to Scott that he had already spent five minutes tamping the black shag into the bowl.

"One time last winter," Beaver began another of his stories, "a pesky wolverine was traveling around my best marten line, springing every trap I set. Then one moonlight night I got to figuring. That critter, I said to myself, is always following along behind you. So I stopped right then and waited down-wind from my last set. Had to wait about six hours, but sure enough, along he came and I knocked him over with one shot."

Tim chuckled. "You and that wolverine going around in circles! Reminds me of the time when Old Pete what's-his-name was hauling the winter mail. Hitched up his dogs one dark morning—got turned around and mushed back along the trail he'd traveled over the day before."

The big man went over and cranked up the battered old gramophone that was on a table in one corner of the room. A husky tenor voice started to blare out: "Dear-r-r Mother-r-r Machree."

"That's real nice," Gee-gee commented. "Better than

that radio the Indian Agent's got. It'd keep a man broke buying batteries for the contraption, and most of the summer you can't hear anything on it anyway."

"Speaking of radio—did you hear that the government was figuring on doing away with the Yukon Telegraph line and putting in wireless stations instead?" Tim set four thick china mugs down on the oilcloth-covered table with a clatter.

"Won't work!" Gee-gee roared. "The Northern Lights play hob with radio. So do the mountains—same as they do with these airplanes that everybody's getting steamed up over." His beard bristled as he fumbled in his pockets for his tobacco sack and started to roll a cigaret.

Tim poured steaming coffee into the mugs and they all pulled their chairs up to the table. Scott sipped at his coffee in silence—what could he say to these old-timers who talked of nothing but the past? It seemed to him that they lived in a world of their own—surrounded by the mountains that they were so sure would shield them from things like radio and planes.

Scott considered going over to the post to have a talk with Jack, but he could think of no polite excuse to offer Tim. Besides, he realized that he might not be welcome while his friend was learning the ropes of his new job.

He turned around eagerly at the sound of a fresh voice. "Hullo this place!" A crisp greeting rose above the noise of the gramophone, and Scott saw a tall, khaki clad figure standing in the doorway.

"Why—hullo, Constable. Come in and have some coffee." Tim gestured toward Scott. "Meet Scott Haliburton—Constable Black."

The constable shook hands with Scott. There was a friendly glow in his dark eyes. "Thanks just the same, Tim, but I'm in a rush to get some reports finished for the mail. Just dropped in to find out what you know about that well-fed looking character with the nugget jewelry who arrived this trip."

Tim shrugged his massive shoulders. "Gold Brick Schnider they call him. Says he's a mining promoter, but not the kind who sits in an office. Claims he gets out in the field and looks things over for himself."

Constable Black smiled as he turned to go. "Thanks— we get all sorts of characters up here, don't we?"

Scott watched the khaki clad figure blend into the gray twilight. The man's words had sounded casual enough. Scott supposed he meant: "All sorts of queer characters." Or was it some other word than "queer" the constable had left unsaid?

Scott shot a glance at the far end of the table. Gee-gee had been sitting there, facing the door. The wrangler's reaction to the constable's brief remark would give him some clue, he thought.

But Gee-gee wasn't there! The only sign of him was a little mound of fine-cut tobacco he had spilled on the floor.

Beaver rose to his feet. "Guess I'll be running along. Looks like Gee-gee went out the back door." He and Tim exchanged a knowing look.

"Same old trouble, I suppose," Tim grunted. "Good night, Beaver."

A few minutes later Scott spread out his new sleeping

bag on a rough wooden bunk built against the wall of the cabin. A smell of newness clung to the eiderdown robe that reminded him of a sporting goods store, with its displays of rifles and fishing tackle. As he settled down for the night, he tried to think of pine woods and clear mountain streams.

But his mind always came back to the questions: "Why had the constable inquired about Gold Brick? Why had Gee-gee disappeared so suddenly?"

And the only answer that he could think of before he dropped off to sleep was that there must be all sorts of queer characters in the Cassiar.

6

SCOTT MEETS THE CAT-SKINNER

Scott opened his eyes and saw Tim methodically sweeping into a dust-pan the fine shreds of tobacco from the scrubbed plank floor of the cabin. For a moment, his mind still fuzzy with sleep, he wondered where all the loose ends of tobacco came from.

Then he remembered last night—Gee-gee sitting at the table, rolling his cigaret in the odd, awkward way he had, using both hands with fingers that seemed to be all thumbs, spilling half his tobacco on the floor.

"May I give you a hand, Tim?"

Tim went on with his sweeping. "No thanks. You take it easy for a while—I have my own way of doing things."

He sure has, Scott decided, and a very exact way it was. At breakfast, he watched the big man pour six circles of batter of exactly the same size onto the hot-cake griddle. When breakfast was over, the dishes had to be washed and put away just so, and shavings left ready to start the fire when they returned. The alarm clock on the shelf pointed to nine o'clock now. Scott wished Tim would get a move on, because he wasn't going to feel things were hunky-dory until he saw the pipe loaded in the freight wagons.

They seemed all ready to leave now, but Tim stopped to examine Scott's sleeping bag. "You're lucky—having your dad buy an outfit like that for you. With a good eiderdown robe and a waterproof groundsheet like this, you'll be comfortable sleeping out in any kind of weather."

Scott sensed mild criticism. The back of his neck prickled. It sounded as if Tim thought he had everything handed to him on a silver platter.

"I paid for part of it with my own money from my paper route," he said—no need to tell just how small that first payment had been. "I'm going to work to pay off the rest when I get to the mine; cutting wood, and . . . well, all sorts of odd jobs, I hope."

"Good for you. You should feel right at home in the Cassiar—working half the season to pay off your 'jaw-bone.' "

Scott knew what Tim meant. Beaver had talked about his "jaw-bone"—the debt he owed for the supplies he bought in the fall. Nice to hear Tim talk like that—sort of made a fellow feel he belonged.

The sun blazed in a topaz sky above the gorge of the Grand Canyon, and long shadows danced on the steep bank beside them as the pair went down the steps to the dock. A grin spread over Scott's face.

"Perhaps I'll find a new prospect and pay for my sleeping bag with gold dust—or even with nuggets," he suggested.

"Why not?" Tim grunted.

Scott didn't answer. Of course they were just kidding. He realized that prospecting called for mature judgment and physical strength, tempered by experience. But everybody said luck played a big part also.

They were on the dock now, and Scott's smile vanished as he noticed that one of the massive, wide-tired freight wagons was already loaded with gasoline drums. The other stood empty, with its tail-gate open, backed up to the gaping door of the warehouse. Inside the building, looming behind the mound of boxes and gunny sacks, Scott saw the black lengths of hydraulic pipe.

Two Indians, dressed in the usual jeans and bright checked shirts, were leaning against the rear wheel of the wagon.

Tim nodded to them. "Gas loaded already—fine, we'll load this wagon with case goods. That will leave about a full load of pipe for the next trip."

Scott gnawed unhappily at his lower lip and felt like kicking himself. He had thought, several times last night, of telling Tim that the pipe had to be loaded first. But he had put it off. Secretly he had hoped that Tim would decide to load the pipe first anyway, and that any chance of an argument would be avoided, if he said nothing beforehand. It had never occurred to him that Tim's helpers would have one wagon loaded before they arrived.

"Just a minute, Tim!" Scott thrust out his lower jaw and hooked his thumbs in his belt. "Dad wants all the pipe to go in this trip, for sure."

Tim turned slowly toward him. He was stroking his

square chin, and a stubborn look was smoldering in his gray eyes. "Come to think of it, he did say something about that in the note I got from him. Well, the way it's turned out, we'll only be able to take half of it this trip."

Scott found it hard to answer without raising his voice. "You'll have to unload those drums of gas and leave them for the next trip. They're setting up another monitor, and they need the pipe right away."

"Well now," Tim drawled, "seems like six of one and half a dozen of the other to me. If they're going to use another monitor, surely they'll be needing more sluice-boxes. And if they're going to cut lumber for sluice-boxes, they'll be using the sawmill. And they can't run that without gas. But, if you say so, we'll leave the gas behind."

Indecision left Scott tongue-tied for a few seconds. His father's letter had said nothing about gasoline—what if Tim were right? Then, suddenly his mind was made up. There was no use wondering and guessing—the letter was the only thing he had to go by—and it said: "Make sure that they bring this pipe in right away."

"Okay." He tried to make it sound as though he were very sure of himself. "That's what you'll have to do—unload the gas drums."

He hardly expected Tim to give in without an argument, but he saw the stubborn set of his jaw relax. The expression in the big man's eyes changed, and he flashed a probing glance at Scott.

The boy felt as though he were standing on air as Tim murmured, "Y'know, I like to see a young fellow who knows his own mind."

"Over here, boys," Tim shouted to his helpers. The dark eyes of the two Indians gleamed at Scott as they set up two thick planks to roll the heavy drums out of the wagon.

Husky looking fellows, these Tahltans, Scott thought, and he grinned back at them as he turned toward the warehouse. "I'll start bringing some of the pipe out," he called to Tim.

Inside the big shed, he discovered Jack standing behind the mound of freight. He had a pencil behind one ear and a sheaf of freight bills in his hand. He was looking very serious, but his eyes brightened at the sight of his friend.

"Hi! You look pleased with yourself," he called.

Scott's grin broadened. "How's it going? You used to tell me I worried too much—now you're the one who looks worried."

"I'm not worrying," Jack countered, "just concentrating. It sure is a heck of a job sorting all this stuff out. Most of this lot will be going down the Dease River to the interior posts."

"Gosh, Jack, it would sure be swell if you were sent in to one of those posts. I should think you'd be able to work in an over-night visit at Osprey Creek on your way downriver."

"Well, keep on wishing—it might work out that way. One of the traders is due out on leave, and the boss is talking about sending me in to relieve him." A smile was flickering across Jack's face now. "You're going to have lots of visitors at the mine, anyway. The constable makes a patrol inside every summer—Gold Brick will be prospecting somewhere in that part of the country and says he plans on making a trip into the mine. Gee-gee is packing some supplies into the Big Muddy country for some prospectors—figures he'll take the trail down Osprey Creek on his way back."

"The more the merrier." Scott walked over and tackled the pile of pipe. It turned out to be much heavier than he had expected. It was all he could manage to pick up a length of it, but it seemed easy enough to roll it along the rough boards of the floor. The first piece reached the gently slanted platform of planks that sloped from the floor of the warehouse to the hard-packed gravel surface of the dock.

Scott felt pleased with himself as he watched the black iron cylinder pick up speed while it trundled down the incline. That was the way to do it—let the law of gravity work for you.

And then, "Hey, look out!" His voice seemed to be drowned out by the rumble of the rolling pipe . . . but it had the desired effect.

The heavy boots and stagged khaki pants that had been standing directly in the path of the pipe stepped back just in time to get out of its way. Stepped back so quickly that the boots tripped on the eight by eight stringer at the edge of the platform, and their owner landed on his back in the sand.

"What in Sam Hill!" It hadn't been a fall of much more than a foot and it didn't take stagged pants long to get on his feet again. "You darned fool, little smart aleck! You might have broken my leg!"

Scott had a blurred impression of a freckled face, dotted in the center with a comical button of a nose, crowned by a shock of flaming red hair. Pale blue eyes seemed to become bloodshot as they drew nearer and to sparkle with fire as they glared at him.

"I'm sorry—honest—it—it was an accident. I—I didn't see you standing there," he stammered.

The worst of it was, Scott reflected unhappily, he had been just plain dumb not to make sure there was no one in the way.

"Now you're sorry!" The redheaded man grabbed him by the front of his shirt. Scott noticed that he was quite young looking; probably in his early twenties.

He twisted back angrily. "Let go—I told you it was an accident—and I told you I was sorry. What more do you want?"

"What more do I want? Huh! 'Tisn't safe to have kids like you fooling around with the freight. I figure what I should do is put you across my knee and give you a good spanking."

Scott glared back at his opponent. They were both about the same height, but the other was stockily built— at least twenty pounds heavier than himself. Scott was scared—really scared, he admitted to himself—but he challenged through clenched teeth: "Take your hands off me! If you won't accept an apology—put up your fists!"

"I don't fight with kids," Red Head snorted without relaxing his grip.

Scott pivoted, ducking one shoulder down in a sudden

violent attempt to wrench himself free. Red Head let go of his shirt and he pitched head first to the ground. He spat out gritty sand as he got up. Come up fighting was all he could think of—but he knew he was bluffing—he was hopelessly outmatched.

Then he was on his feet. There was his opponent, standing with his hands in his pockets—and there was Tim, strolling over toward them.

"Was just coming over to introduce you two." Tim stopped to look at them with his hands on his hips. "Say —what kind of shenanigans have you been up to?"

A scowl from Red Head. A shrug of the shoulders from Scott. Tim had saved his bacon this time, but he was darned if he was going to tell him what had happened.

This was something he would have to get out of by himself.

"Just playing around," he mumbled, trying hard to smile.

"Looks like you were playing pretty rough. Your arm is bleeding, you must have hit the gravel pretty hard." Tim looked quizzically from one to the other. "I suppose you've introduced yourselves then."

Scott shot a glance at Red Head. It was all beginning to seem rather silly now. He hoped to see some trace of a smile on that freckled face, but it was still sullen and scowling. He answered Tim with a very faint, "No."

"Sure now, it will be a great privilege for me to do the honors then. On my left hand, wearing tin pants: Bunny, the cat-skinner. Undefeated holder of the Cassiar grouch title. On my right hand, wearing blue jeans: Scott Haliburton, leaving tomorrow for Osprey Creek."

So Red Head was the cat-skinner! The driver of the tractor train! What kind of a trip was it going to be?

Instinctively, Scott took a step forward and prepared to shake hands, but Bunny remained with his hands in his pockets and the scowl still on his face. "So his old man owns a gold mine? Well—you can't expect me to take a youngster like that over the trail. There's no first-class accommodation on a cat-train. Has he got a bedroll?"

"Sure I have!" Scott could feel the flush of anger crawl up the back of his neck again. "And you can leave my dad out of this. I'm going in to the mine to work, and I'll travel just the same as the rest of the gang."

"Hah!" Bunny kicked a pebble into the river without taking his hands from his pockets. "Have you got a mosquito tent? You'll be eaten alive at nights if you haven't."

"Well . . ." Scott wasn't so sure of himself now. But Tim put in quickly, "I'll soon fix you up with one—just a sort of pup tent with cheesecloth sides—that's all it is."

Scott grinned—Tim had certainly brushed that problem aside easily, and as far as Tim was concerned, everything seemed to be settled.

The big man turned briskly to Bunny. "You'd better check the brakes on the wagons after you're through with the cat. Full load of pipe this time, with some groceries on top of it. You'll sure need brakes on those hills this trip."

Bunny growled, "That's haywire—loading the wagons top-heavy like that. It's tough enough with an ordinary load, the way the trail is just now. Dust that grinds heck out of the machinery for the first twenty miles, and then mud up to the axles from Tuya Bridge to the Lake."

Tim shrugged his massive shoulders and chuckled. "Cheer up! If it wasn't for the mud and the steep grades, you'd be driving a truck, instead of drawing cat-skinner's wages."

Bunny snorted and clattered up the steps, saying something about going to grease up.

"Don't forget what I said about the brakes," Tim called after him. Then he turned to Scott. "How about you rolling the pipe out? The Indians and I will load it on the wagons."

"Sure!" Scott was pleased at the idea of helping with the job. He headed back to the warehouse, where he met Jack coming out.

"All there, after all." Jack fluttered the freight bills in his hand. "What was the argument about? It burnt me up that I couldn't hear what was going on."

"Tell you about it later." Scott went in to tackle the stack of pipe. He trundled the heavy lengths across the floor and let them coast down the ramp to where Tim and the Indians were waiting to roll them up thick planks into the wagons.

When the pipe was loaded, Tim announced it was time to knock off for lunch. After lunch, they started boosting boxes and gunny sacks over the edges of the wagon-boxes. It was hard work, but Scott was determined to do his share.

The afternoon sun blazed down on the dock. Scott stripped off his shirt. Beads of perspiration trickled down his chest and back. But there was satisfaction in working side by side with grown men, even if he was sticky and dusty and even though his arms and shoulders ached from the heavy lifting.

At last Tim said, "That's the lot. Five tons in each wagon. Now the tarps and we'll be through."

They spread heavy canvas covers over the cargo and lashed them down; the pipe was loaded and the wagons were all ready to start over the trail in the morning.

"All hunky-dory!" Scott thought as he pulled on his shirt. Then he heard Jack hailing him from the top of the steps. "Hey there! Are you all in? Or would you like to come for a walk up the creek? I have to go up to clear the intake of our water system."

Tim said, "Go ahead. It'll only take a few minutes and it's two hours till dinner time."

"Okay! I'll be right with you." Scott climbed the steps and he and Jack walked up the road past Tim's cabin. It led them into the cleft where the creek flowed through the cliffs that bordered the settlement. After ten minutes they came to a wooden tank, about five feet square, into which water from the creek was fed by a short wooden flume.

Jack balanced on the rocks at the edge of the creek and reached down. "Looks simple enough. I lift the trough out and we wait until the tank drains so we can clear the leaves and twigs from the screens."

Scott stepped down from the road and peered into the tank. For a minute or two he studied with amusement the distorted image of his face mirrored in the dark, rippled water. Then, uncannily, another face appeared beside his.

"Hi!" Scott wheeled around, but there was no answer. He gazed in bewilderment at the back of a dark-haired, thickset man, hurrying on down the trail.

The stranger vanished around a bend and Scott turned in the other direction to see Jack climbing back onto the road. "Now we take it easy until the water goes down. Say! Did you see a ghost?"

Scott forced a smile. "I guess not. It was a real, live Indian as far as I could tell. He seemed to bob up behind me from nowhere. All I saw was the reflection of his face in the tank, and then his back disappearing down the trail. Gave me a sort of a start—he didn't make a sound."

Jack shrugged. "Guess he was wearing moccasins."

"I suppose so," Scott agreed. "Queer he wouldn't speak to me. Just as queer as something that happened at Tim's cabin last night."

"What was that?"

"Beaver and Gee-gee were dishing out some mighty tall stories when the constable looked in to ask Tim if he knew who Gold Brick was. Gee-gee didn't say a word, but apparently he slipped out the back door."

"*Hm-m,* he's a queer old duck," Jack mused. "Say! You were going to tell me about the rumpus on the dock."

"Well, I rolled a length of pipe down the ramp and it nearly hit that redheaded cat-skinner—Bunny they call him. He got sore and grabbed hold of me and I offered to take him on. I guess it's lucky for me that Tim came along and calmed him down. Bunny doesn't act as though he's going to forget it though. I'm not looking forward to three days on the trail with him."

"Worry-wart!" Jack chuckled. "So he has a chip on his shoulder? You won't need to knock it off—the first few hours bumping over that trail will do that. Things will look a lot different when there's just three of you camping out under the stars. You'll be okay."

"I guess you're right," Scott admitted. Jack's banter always seemed to renew his confidence in himself.

Jack looked in the tank. "We can go to work now." A few minutes later he set the flume back in place and the two boys started back toward the river.

A rubble of sharp fragments of gray-green rock bordered the road. Scott picked up a small piece of it and put it in his pocket.

Jack murmured, "Lots more where that came from. I I thought you'd have your eye on it, so I asked about it. The folks around here call it lava rock."

"Lava—that covers a lot of territory." Scott didn't want to sound as if he were showing off, so he said no more. It was volcanic rock, all right—some type of basalt, he supposed—he could find out for sure later.

"You mean just plain lava rock isn't scientific enough for you? What are you going to label it then?" Jack asked.

They were almost at Tim's cabin now. A few hundred yards on his left, Scott could see the beginning of the Cassiar Trail. It was blasted out of a cliff of the same type of rock that he had in his pocket.

Scott looked at Jack and grinned. "There are a lot of things I don't know yet. I'll just call this sample, 'Cassiar Number One.' "

7

DISASTER AT TUYA CANYON

THE crackling cough of the cat's engine surged up from the dock. The noise seemed to bounce back from the rocks of the cliffs and fill the narrow valley with a stormy sea of sound.

Scott swung his dunnage bag over his shoulder and jogged down the steps two at a time.

"You've got plenty of time," called out Tim, who was following behind him with his bedroll.

Gosh! Had Tim ever been slow, straightening things up after breakfast? It had begun to seem as though they never would get started, Scott thought. He didn't slow-up, for he was determined not to give Bunny a chance to say he was holding up the start of the cat-train.

He smiled and nodded at Bunny as he arrived on the dock. But all he received in reply was a downward twitch of the lips. The cat-skinner was concentrating on backing his machine into place to couple onto the lead-wagon. It took just the right pressure on the two levers he held in his hands to do it. Finally—after the cat had wiggled from side to side several times—Tim held the wagon tongue in place while the Indian swamper slipped in the heavy coupling pin.

The swamper climbed on the wagon and signaled for Scott to heave his dunnage up. Above him, Scott noticed the pale yellow orb of the morning sun shining through thin, high clouds scudding eastward. Sounding far away, he heard Tim's voice over the roar of the idling engine. "Nice day for it, Bunny. Not too hot and she doesn't look like rain."

"Huh! Nice day for you, all right, sitting pretty in this dump where it never does rain. See the way those clouds are heading—we'll catch up with them before we cross the Tuya. Might as well get started, though. Boost that kid up on the wagon and we'll get going."

So—Bunny still had a chip on his shoulder. Scott wasn't going to have anyone helping him up. He gripped the spokes of the hind wheel and clambered up until he could reach the lash-rope at the edge of the wagon box. He would have made it easily if he hadn't been in such a rush. But when he gave a hefty heave that should have landed him on top of the load, his foot slipped off the smooth steel tire of the wheel.

The swamper grabbed his arm and saved him from falling. "Your leg hurt?"

"No!" Scott felt as though his shin were afire, but the physical pain was nothing compared to the realization that Bunny had witnessed his clumsiness. He saw the cat-skinner look at Tim and shrug his shoulders, as though he were saying, "I told you so."

Scott's ears started to burn with humiliation, but he squared his jaw and said to himself, "I'll show him."

Tim waved and shouted to them, but his farewell was drowned out by the roar of the cat and the crunch of wheels on gravel as the loaded wagons jostled ahead. Two other figures at the edge of the terrace above them were waving good-bye. There was a lump in Scott's throat as he caught sight of Jack and Beaver. Even old Dinty, standing between them, seemed to be trying to say good-bye also, by swishing his scrawny tail to and fro.

Five noisy minutes rolled under the tracks of the cat and the figures of those Scott had come to know as friends faded into the distance behind him. He felt very much alone as they crawled into the shadows under an overhanging wall of rock. But he snapped out of his melancholy mood as he helped the swamper arrange the loose dunnage on top of the load to make a comfortable place to sit.

"Your name is Scott—eh? Mine's Jim—Jim Brokenose."

Scott brightened up. "Pleased to meet you, Jim. But you don't look as if you'd ever had a broken nose."

Jim's lips drew back in a smile, exposing an even row of gleaming white teeth. "I'm Tom Brokenose's son. My grandfather doesn't like that name, though. He likes to stick to his Tahltan name."

"What was that?"

"Thlon-on-etze." Jim's lips scarcely moved. "You can't say that, though. If you try, pretty soon it will sound like Brokenose."

"Well, does it mean Brokenose in English?"

"No." Jim's face suddenly became a blank. "My grandfather was a chief. His name had something to do with fighting, I guess."

"But don't you know what his name meant?" Scott persisted.

"He's old-fashioned, that's all I know. We don't go for that old stuff any more." Jim started to smile again and settled back against the dunnage. "Pretty soft—eh?"

It sure was, Scott decided. You had a better view than you'd have from the observation car of a train. Of course, it was bumpy and the dust and exhaust fumes blowing back from the cat got into your eyes, up your nose and down your throat. And slow! Golly! A fellow could walk as fast as the wagons were going. But what of it? All the more chance to see the country.

New country it was, to Scott. They had climbed to a bench high above the settlement. The river foamed through a narrow canyon far below them. From this height it looked like tufts of wool threaded on a silver ribbon. On the other side of the trail were rounded hills, with pines and aspens at their feet. The southern slopes of the hills were bare, except for withered, yellow tufts of bunch grass and drab patches of sagebrush. Dry-belt country. Scott had never seen anything like it before.

Two round, white boulders stood out against the reddish soil on one of the side-hills. Where had these lone rocks come from? Had they been left in the path of a melting glacier, thousands of years ago? Some day Scott hoped he would be able to answer questions like these.

Dusty miles slipped slowly behind them along the red ruts of the dust track curving into the pines. Close to midday, they emerged from the friendly green of the woods and started down a long, steep hill. Here the road had been blasted out of solid rock and the jagged face of the cliff loomed on their left. On the other side, the sheer wall of the canyon seemed to lean outward over the river.

Jim tugged with all his might at the two ropes attached to the brake levers. "Pretty soft—eh? All I have to do is pull like the dickens."

The brake shoes screeched like beings in torment as they gripped the steel clad wheels. Scott remembered Tim's warning on the dock: "You'll sure need brakes on those hills this trip." They hadn't meant much to him at the time.

Now, with the heavy wagons fighting to free themselves of the drag of the brakes, Tim's words revolved in his head—as though a gramophone had stuck on one groove. "You'll sure need brakes! You'll sure need brakes!" Scott could sense the powerful thrust of the ten-ton load. It seemed like a living monster, eager to push the crawling cat to one side in its rush downhill.

Ten minutes later the wagons jerked to a stop beside a clump of willows obstinately rooted in a gravel flat at the bank of a small river. Bunny switched off the ignition and climbed stiffly to the ground. He stretched a couple of times, then flung himself down with his back against a log.

"Lunch time now, I guess." Jim loosened a lash-rope and started to pull out a big grub-box.

Scott stepped on the hub of the front wheel and jumped lightly to the gravel. He sniffed the air with relish. A brisk breeze rustled through the willows and brought with it a clean, woodsy tang to replace the stench of exhaust fumes. It also seemed to waft away most of the resentment against Bunny that still lingered in his mind. He shot a quick glance at the cat-skinner. Why shouldn't they get on with each other?

Bunny had his hands clasped behind his head and was twisting his neck back and forth. "What a life!" he complained to the cliffs across the river. He didn't appear to notice that Scott was there. "That ring-dinged cat rattles your insides around and just about jars your head loose from your shoulders."

Scott looked about and saw that this was evidently a regular stopping place. There was a crude fireplace of smoke blackened rocks and a few sticks of dry wood piled beside it. He snapped open his Scout knife. He was proud of the razor edge he always kept honed on the blade.

This was a moment he had been waiting for. Scott started to peel off long, curly pine shavings. He'd show Bunny he could build a fire.

"What in Sam Hill are you up to?" Bunny snapped.

"Thought I'd get a fire going while Jim was fetching the grub-box." Scott didn't look around.

"Humpf!" Bunny was on his feet now. He stamped over to the cat and came back with a tin in his hand. He kicked a few sticks of wood into the fireplace, drenched them with gasoline and struck a match on the seat of his pants.

"We don't have time to play Boy Scouts on this job," Bunny growled as he dodged back from the flame that spurted up.

Scott snapped his knife shut and thrust out his lower lip. "That's a good way to singe your eyebrows!"

"Not if you know what you're doing."

Scott thought maybe there was something in what Bunny said, if you were in a hurry, if you were used to handling gas. It was a haywire way of doing things, but no use starting an argument about it.

Jim set the grub-box down with a clatter and started to read out the labels on the cans. "What'll it be? We have Irish Stew, Beef Steak and Gravy."

"What does it matter?" Bunny propped himself against the log again. "Mix them all up together—they all taste the same, anyway."

Jim went to work with the can opener. "Never mind, Bunny. My folks are hunting somewhere around Caribou Camp. Maybe we'll have moose steaks tomorrow."

Scott was surprised at Bunny's reply. "Say! That would be dandy." Surely it was the first time he'd heard the cat-skinner approve of anything.

As Jim started to clean out the frying pan, when they had finished eating, he said, "Guess we'll have to relay the wagons."

Scott gazed across the river at the trail that slanted steeply up the cliffs from a sun-bleached bridge. He could understand why the cat would only be able to haul one wagon at a time up a grade like that.

"Yeah." Bunny looked at Scott without smiling. "We

won't need your help. You could walk on ahead and we'll catch up to you later. That is, if you're not afraid of being in the woods alone."

Scott snorted. "Nuts! What is there to be afraid of?" He started toward the river.

Bunny called after him, "You may find out!"

Scott quickened his pace and the weathered planking of the bridge rang under his footsteps. I'll show Bunny he can't razz me, he thought. I know from what Tim and Gee-gee said, this isn't grizzly country.

Ahead of him, he could count five distinct layers of rock in the canyon wall; but when he drew closer, the colors blended into a uniform drab green. Sweltering in the sun's heat, reflected from the rocks, he started the steep climb.

Soon he was out of sight of the camp. It was lonesome on this bare, rocky road, he had to admit. It would be a swell walk, though, if Jack were along. Good old Jack! He always seemed to have such good sense about things. But Jack had been wrong about Bunny. Jolting over the trail certainly hadn't knocked the chip off the cat-skinner's shoulder. That crack about the Scouts when Scott prepared to light the fire had been hard to take.

Thinking about this turned Scott's thoughts back to Captain Dan. He had been ungrudging in his approval of the Scouts' training. Perhaps Scott should have told him about the loss of his rock samples. Too late to worry about that now, though. *Remember the Jack o' Diamonds claim*—that's what he had to keep in his mind.

Scott stopped to break off a small sample of rock by hurling a slab onto the roadway. He decided he should have a geologist's hammer for jobs like this. There would be one at Osprey Creek . . . three more days . . . surely nothing could happen to make it longer. . . . Scott plodded on up the hill.

When he reached the top, all thoughts of the past or future were swept from his mind by the breathtaking panorama of mountains and valley. Hundreds of feet below him, the river he had just crossed joined the Stikine in a smother of foam that disappeared into a deep canyon.

He stood for five minutes, drinking in the immensity of the chasm below and savoring the grandeur of the mountains in the distance. Then he turned on his heels and headed along the trail.

He found himself amongst pine woods where the only underbrush was an occasional clump of saskatoon bushes. This was certainly different from the devil's-club he and Jack had struggled through at the Boundary. Remembering Gee-gee's advice, Scott whistled and clicked his heels on the road. He swept a casual glance over the plants carpeting the ground among the trees. Something red and appetizing looking caught his eye and he stooped down to investigate. "Wow!" He spoke aloud. "Wild strawberries—here's where I have a feed!"

The tiny berries melted in his mouth. He could faintly hear the cat in the distance now—a gentle purr creeping up the cliffs. There was no other sound, but some sixth sense made him look up.

The hair prickled on Scott's scalp. A great, dark form loomed through the pines. It looked as big as an elephant! For a fleeting moment he thought the long head turned toward him had four ears—and then he realized that it was a bull moose, with half-grown horns still in the velvet.

Scott sprang to his feet, waving his arms and yelling, "Yah-o-o! Waho-o-o!"

The great beast wheeled away from him. Picking up its long legs with surprising grace, it disappeared into the forest without making a sound. Only after it had gone did Scott's heart begin to pound. Oddly, the thing that seemed most frightening was that such a huge animal could move through the woods without snapping a twig.

Scott started to whistle again and kept it up until the cat-train stopped to pick him up.

"Golly! Jim, I saw a bull moose. I yelled at him and he ran away . . . but wow! He looked big!"

Jim settled back against the dunnage. "Two-year-old, I guess. The big bulls won't be moving around much until fall time. Then they don't always run away from you."

Scott was silent. Jim should know what he was talking about. One thing Scott was sure of—he didn't want to be close to any animal that big if it didn't run away.

For two hours the wagons clattered and clanked along a fairly level trail through the woods. Then they started down a gentle slope. A valley about half a mile across, shaped like a flat bowl, appeared below them. Beyond it, Scott saw the road continuing steeply up across the flank of a dome-shaped hill. Jim pointed to the right. "Alf Hodgin's farm."

Scott could hardly believe his eyes as the checkerboard fields came into view. It seemed like a mirage—an oasis in the wilderness. He saw rows of potatoes, carrots and turnips, underlined here and there by small irrigation ditches. There was a green field that looked like oats, but the only livestock in sight were two chestnut horses, grazing in a distant patch of pasture.

The cat neared the pole gate at the entrance to the farm. Jim exclaimed, "Golly! Look at that truck! Wonder where Alf is, maybe he's . . ."

Scott looked around quickly and saw a light pickup truck almost turned on its side and half buried in one of the ditches, just inside the gate. For a moment he wondered if Alf was trapped in the cab—a man could get knocked out in an upset like that . . . but this must be Alf coming out of the house now.

Alf was leaning on the gate by the time Bunny shut off the engine. "Dagnabbed ditch caved in! Those horses of mine have too much bronc in 'em to do any pulling. You got time to give 'er a tug?"

Bunny nodded. "Sure thing!" But Scott jumped down and rushed up to the cat. All he could think was: "We've got to keep going! We'll never get the pipe in, if we fool around like this!"

Scott faced Bunny squarely. "This load of pipe has to get in! You can pull his truck out on the way back."

"The heck with 'on the way back,'" Bunny snapped. "Can't leave a guy in the lurch like that. Jim! Uncouple the wagons."

Scott stepped back, speechless with rage. Dumbly, he watched Jim hook a wire choker from the cat to the axle of the truck. Then he gradually forgot his anger as he added his weight to that of Jim and Alf while they bore down on a stout pole to pry the truck up when the cat pulled.

It took a much shorter time than Scott had expected. He began to feel sorry he had tried to interfere. He supposed that would be another thing Bunny would hold against him.

It seemed no time at all before they were on their way again. Over the crest of the hill, the wagon wheels cut into sticky gray mud. Brown water in the ruts showed there had been a heavy rainfall not long ago.

Banks of clouds blotted out the sun. Scott pulled on his jacket and asked, "When do we eat?"

Jim said, "As soon as we get across the Tuya. We're just coming to the canyon."

Scott looked down into a narrow defile where all the brightness of the sky seemed to have disappeared. All the green seemed to have vanished from the spruce and pines in the great gorge. It looked black, somber and menacing.

The brake shoes seemed to screech in protest at the heavy load as the cat-train started its lumbering descent into the twilight of the canyon. On one side was a wall of naked clay from which the road had been gouged. Scott gripped the lash-ropes and looked over the outside edge of the wagon. Close below him was a steep bank, with scattered trees rooted between outcroppings of jagged rock. Far beneath was the burnished steel thread of the Tuya, winding between tree-lined banks.

For a minute or so Scott was held spellbound, gazing at the sheer drop below them. Then, suddenly, an urgent note of bewilderment and anxiety in Jim's voice made him wheel around.

"Rope . . . seems to be stretching. . . . Give me a hand—quick!"

Scott twisted on his haunches, took hold of the rear brake-rope and added his weight to Jim's. A split-second later, they landed together in a heap amongst the loose dunnage.

The rope had snapped! Before they could scramble to their feet, Scott felt the sudden surge as the five-ton load behind them lunged ahead, uncontrolled.

They could still use the brakes on the first wagon, but Scott knew they couldn't possibly hold back the plunging weight behind. He measured the distance between the two wagons with his eye and for a moment considered trying to jump across so he could work the rear brake lever by hand. But he saw he couldn't possibly make it. Glancing forward, he saw that the sudden thrust ahead had reached the cat.

Bunny lifted one hand from a control lever long enough to signal for them to jump. Scott and Jim landed beside each other in the mud.

His breath almost knocked out of him, Scott was up in time to see the rear wagon wheels squelching past him. Bunny was still on the cat, looking straight ahead.

"Bunny! Jump! Jump before it's too late!" But Scott's shout was drowned in the noise of the engine.

He could tell from the sound that Bunny had "given her the gun." He realized the cat-skinner was taking a desperate chance—trying to drive the cat fast enough to keep ahead of the uncontrolled wagons.

But the rear wagon forced the one ahead toward the edge of the precipice. Then the wagons folded together like a jackknife and disappeared over the bank with a sickening crash of splintering wood.

Scott tried to run but his legs felt heavy as lead. He saw the cat poised briefly on the edge after the wagons went over. Then it, too, disappeared. Bunny was still clutching the levers.

The roar of the engine was snuffed out. There was an eerie silence, broken only by the sound of things sliding down the side-hill. There was a metallic clang, mingled with the noises that seemed to Scott to be sounding the death knell of the precious pipe that was so badly needed at the mine.

Scott's knees wobbled as though they were made of rubber as he stood peering down into the canyon. Suddenly, he felt as though he were going to be sick.

"Jim! I can see Bunny. . . . He's lying against a rock. . . . He . . . he . . . he's not moving!"

8

SCOTT'S VIGIL IN THE NIGHT

TWENTY feet to go! Not more. But twenty feet straight down the face of the cliff to the narrow ledge where Bunny lay sprawled! The tips of Scott's fingers were scraped and bleeding from clutching at jagged points of rock during the time it took to cover the distance. And there was Bunny, his face covered with blood and one leg twisted underneath him, with the foot turned sideways in a sickening, unnatural fashion.

This was no mock accident, like those Scott had treated when he took his first-aid course. This was the real thing. He must keep cool. But, in spite of himself, his head reeled when he saw the red blood pumping from a gash in Bunny's forearm.

Scott was conscious of Jimmy Brokenose standing behind him, his face gray as a ghost in the shadows. Somehow it gave him confidence to realize that the Indian was waiting for him to do something. He pulled himself together and clamped his fingers firmly on the pressure point in Bunny's upper arm. Almost at once, the crimson spurting stopped. Scott nearly sobbed with relief.

"Give me your neckerchief," he muttered tersely to Jim. He clamped the cloth against the wound and before long the arterial bleeding was stopped. What next? "Treat for shock." Scott could hear his scoutmaster's words. He turned to Jim.

"Did the cat carry a first-aid kit?"

"Sure thing!"

"We'll have to get the kit and some bed-rolls up from the wreck."

"I'll get them." And the Indian disappeared into the gorge.

When Jim returned, Scott asked him to hand him a compress and antiseptic from the kit. Releasing his firm hold on the wound, he saw that the blood had clotted. Quickly he applied disinfectant to the open gash, placed the compress over it and bandaged it firmly with clean gauze.

Then Scott began a careful examination of his patient. The blood on Bunny's face was from superficial cuts. There was no bleeding from the mouth or ears to indicate internal injuries. Scott loosened the cat-skinner's belt, cut his shoelaces and gently drew off the heavy boots. Then he slit the right trouser leg. A black and blue lump, as big as an egg, in the center of the shin and the foot flopping over like part of a marionette told their own story.

"His leg's broken. . . . A fracture case shouldn't be moved until the doctor arrives." Scott shivered. No telling when that would be! There was nothing for it. Scott would have to take the responsibility. The leg would have to be splinted before Bunny was moved. . . . That twisted foot . . . would it be hard to straighten?

Scott pointed at Bunny's leg. "See if you can find some small pieces of board, Jim—we'll have to attend to that before we cover him."

Jim didn't have far to search in the wake of the shattered wagons to find something that would do. Scott sat down and grasped Bunny's foot. The boy was trembling a little. "Careful not to use force." Again he could hear his scoutmaster speaking. But a nagging voice inside Scott kept asking, "What if the foot won't move without using force?"

But a gentle pull on the foot and it started to move. "Slowly does it," he thought. There was a faint, sickening grinding from the broken ends of the bone that seemed to stab through to the pit of Scott's stomach—and then he held the leg in a normal position.

"Hurry, Jim!" Sudden relaxing of the nervous strain made Scott's voice high-pitched. "Hold the splints on— easy now—have to have something to tie them with. No! Not the bandages from the kit—they're too precious for that. We'll use those straps off the bed-rolls."

Scott moved up to tie the splints himself. So far so good, he said to himself. But how hard is it going to be to move him into a comfortable position?

Scott stood up and shot a quick glance around the ledge. "Jim, we'll spread one eiderdown out here. Thanks — that's it—his feet should be higher than his head. That's the idea. Now help me move Bunny. Careful! Careful! You take his shoulders—I'll watch this leg. We don't want to have anything else happen to it!"

At last they had Bunny lying on his back on the eiderdown. Scott covered him with the other robe. There was time to think now. "How long would it take you to get into Telegraph Creek for the doctor, Jim?" he asked.

The Indian was starting to collect wood for a fire. "I can have him here some time in the morning. Alf will be able to run me in with his truck."

For a moment Scott couldn't meet Jim's eyes. "The truck!" It would save Jim a twenty-mile hike. . . . Lucky thing Bunny hadn't listened to Scott about leaving it in the ditch until the return trip!

The fire was crackling now. Jim said, "Before I start, I'd better go down to the wreck and bring up a mosquito-tent, an ax, some grub and some cooking pots."

"Good idea!" To Scott the minutes seemed to drag by until Jim returned. He broke off what dry lower branches he could, to keep the fire going. Several times he bent down to feel Bunny's feeble pulse. The cat-skinner was still unconscious.

But at last Jim was back. "There's a spring a little way along the bank," he said. "I'll fill the kettles."

Scott used the first water they boiled to sponge off Bunny's face. While he was doing this the cat-skinner's eyelids flickered. A feeling of relief surged in the boy's breast as he heard his patient murmur, "How're things going, Scott?"

"Just fine, Bunny. Everything's going to be all right," Scott answered. To himself he said, "That's the first time he's called me by name." Then he called out, "Jim, how's the coffee coming?"

"Coffee coming up in about five minutes," Jim sang out.

Scott saw that Bunny appeared to be unconscious again. He helped the swamper rig the mosquito tent over the patient. Then the boy knelt down beside Bunny and saw a slight flush of color replacing the grayness in his face. The cat-skinner seemed to be completely conscious now. Scott raised his head and gave him sips of hot black coffee. Suddenly, brightness gleamed in Bunny's eyes and he made a feeble attempt to sit up, but Scott held him by the shoulder.

"Remember what happened now . . . let her jack-knife on me," the cat-skinner muttered. "Where's Jim?"

"Jim's okay. He's going in for the doctor as soon as he's had something to eat."

"I'm leaving right now." Jim's head appeared under the tent-flap for a moment.

"Good luck, Jim!" Scott turned his attention to his patient. "Tell me how you're feeling, Bunny."

"Well . . . feels like a log lying on top of my leg . . . and my face . . . sore as blazes. Feels like somebody jabbed me with a branding iron. . . ."

"Sure that's all? Does this hurt? Feel any pain inside?" Scott pressed Bunny lightly in the ribs and chest.

"No! Heck! I'll be up and around in a few minutes."

Scott tried to make his voice sound stern. "No, you won't! You have a broken leg and you've lost a lot of blood—severed an artery in your arm. You're going to lie still until Jim gets back with the doctor. I'm going to fix up something hot for you to drink."

Scott crawled under the tent flap and looked over the cans the swamper had brought up. He opened two marked *oxtail soup* and heated their contents in the kettle.

When he came back into the tent with a mug of hot broth, the chalky whiteness of Bunny's face sent a chill up the boy's spine. He groped for his patient's wrist to feel his pulse. For a few seconds he had difficulty in detecting it because it was so weak. And when he did feel its throb, it seemed rapid and irregular—like a kicker with faulty spark plugs.

Bunny's teeth were chattering, but Scott managed to feed him sips of hot soup. He took a warm stone from near the fire, wrapped it in canvas, and placed it against the patient's feet.

In a few minutes, Bunny stopped shivering. He murmured, "Sorry . . . felt kind of funny . . . better now." Scott supported his head and held another mug of steaming broth to his lips.

Bunny whispered, "Thanks . . . sure hits the spot." Scott allowed his head to sink back onto the eiderdown and the cat-skinner fell asleep almost immediately. The boy heaved a great sigh of relief. His patient was breathing naturally and evenly and his pulse and temperature seemed to be normal.

Scott suddenly felt desperately tired. But he must stay awake! He must stay awake to keep an eye on Bunny. He huddled before the fire with his chin on his knees, getting up every few minutes to fetch more wood.

Overhead, a pale yellow moon shimmered through layers of thin, gray clouds. All around him, trees and rocks took on fantastic forms in the eerie twilight. Close by, an owl hooted at intervals and from far up the valley, Scott heard shrill yapping howls. Coyotes or foxes, he supposed, as he stared drowsily into the waning fire.

The flames died down to red coals. The shrill yelping stopped. Even the owl seemed to have gone to sleep. Scott told himself: Next time it hoots, I'll get up for more wood. But the valley seemed wrapped in a blanket of silence and the circle of glowing embers grew smaller as he waited.

Suddenly the valley was filled with a sound that froze the marrow in Scott's bones. There was no doubt in his mind as to what it was. The howl of the timber wolf!

Each time the deep-throated, savagely terrifying sound echoed afresh from the canyon walls, it drew closer.

Scott blew on the embers and frantically tried to fan them into flames. He heard the wolves coming straight down the valley. They were directly below him.

There was a sudden flurry of snarling and the click of stones on the sidehill. He could only imagine what was happening. The wolf-pack must have been on the trail of game down in the canyon. Now, frightened by the scent of the wreckage, they were coming up hill. The boy tried to reassure himself by remembering how trappers and woodsmen laughed at the stories of wolves attacking men. But he couldn't help shuddering.

Wolves were afraid of fire. But he had let the fire go down! From below the ledge, the wolves wouldn't see the glow of red coals. But they would have the scent of fresh blood in their nostrils. He could hear them howling now, only a few yards down the hill.

Some of the twigs he had piled on the ashes flickered into a tiny flame. Scott grabbed a branch of green pine and held it in the fire. As the resinous needles flared up, he hurled the flaming torch over the ledge. It burned just long enough to reflect three pairs of yellow eyes and to give him a glimpse of dark forms disappearing into the blackness of the canyon.

It was like a nightmare, he thought, as he piled fresh wood on the fire. He fought off his sleepiness and made sure that the crackling flames from the pine logs didn't die down. Hour after hour dragged by until, at last, gray light filtered down into the gorge. Below him, blurred shapes started to emerge as trees and rocks.

Scott crept into the tent to find that Bunny was wide-awake.

"Well, Scott, how're we doing?"

"Jake-a-loo, Bunny. How d'you feel?"

"Just fine—except my leg's mighty stiff. . . . Say! You look sleepy. Don't tell me you've been up all night. Heck! Guess you were because I have all the sleeping robes. I'm plenty warm now—grab this top robe and roll yourself up for a bit of shut-eye."

Scott drew the sleeping bag around him. "You wake me up if you want anything—and don't try to sit up."

"Don't worry! You go ahead and grab some sleep."

"Have you been asleep all the time, Bunny? Didn't you hear any noise during the night?"

"Nope! Don't tell me one of those side-hill gougers came nosing around."

Scott stifled a yawn. "Do they have long bushy tails, howl like banshees and travel up and down hill so fast you can hardly see them?"

"Yep—that's right."

"That's what they were then. There were at least three of them."

Bunny tried to twist his head so he could see Scott's face. "Hey! Wait a minute. Who's kidding whom around this camp?"

The cat-skinner was left to figure out the answer for himself because Scott was fast asleep.

Scott didn't stir until late in the forenoon, when a truck horn honked at the top of the hill. Instantly he was wide-awake.

By the time the doctor reached the ledge, fresh wood crackled on the fire. With a nod to Scott, he proceeded to examine Bunny, asking questions as he did so. How long had the patient been unconscious? Had he been moved before his leg was splinted?

Scott made his answers brief and to the point. The doctor's terse voice didn't invite long explanations. The boy began to wonder if he had made some stupid mistakes. If he had, he wished the doctor would say so instead of just murmuring: *"U-u-m h-u-mf,"* when he answered the questions.

Out of the corner of his eye, Scott saw Tim Donovan and Constable Black in the background. The constable pointed downhill and they disappeared below the ledge.

At last the doctor stood up and faced Scott. "Where

did you learn so much about first-aid?" he asked quietly.

Over the doctor's shoulder, Scott saw Tim and the constable returning to the ledge. Something in the doctor's expression told him he had nothing to worry about. "I was lucky enough to be on the first-aid team that won the provincial trophy for our Scout troop this spring."

"Well—this cat-skinner was certainly lucky you were with him this trip. I wish all my accident cases could be handled like this one was."

The doctor had raised his voice. Scott knew that Bunny must have heard the verdict. Apparently Tim and the constable had also.

Constable Black echoed, "Lucky is right! Lucky in more ways than one. We've just been looking at fresh wolf tracks less than fifty feet below."

Scott felt that all eyes were fixed on him. "They soon ran away when I threw a torch at them."

Tim nodded. "The burnt branch—the tracks in the clay. It was all as plain as the nose on your face. And I'm the one that understands. Sure, there's nothing makes a man feel so alone as the wolves howling close to camp at night."

"Gosh all hemlock! And I thought he was kidding." Bunny's voice came from the stretcher. "Scott, you've sure got what it takes!"

Everyone appreciated what Scott had done. The knowledge should have made up for the long vigil of the night. But there was a question running through his head that made his mind spin. While he had been looking after

Bunny, he had managed not to worry about the answer.

A voice inside Scott was asking, "How long will it take to get the wagon-train on the trail again? How long will it take to get the pipe into the mine?"

9

"NOT A WORD ABOUT THIS
TO ANYONE!"

THERE was still the difficult task ahead of getting the stretcher up to the road. Scott's training had taught him that he ought not leave Bunny now, even though a doctor was on the scene. But he couldn't help thinking impatiently to himself, "If I could only have a look at the wreck—perhaps I could tell if the wagons can be repaired. I could see what shape the pipe is in, if nothing else."

Above him he heard Tim shout, "This rope in the truck will be too short to reach the stretcher."

The doctor asked, "How about the brake-ropes from the wagons?"

"Fine! Just what the doctor ordered!" The constable laughed and started over the ledge.

Scott climbed down behind him. This was his chance to inspect the wreck, and it was all part of looking after his patient. "I'll give you a hand. Jim told me the easiest way to get down," the boy explained.

Scott and Constable Black slithered down the loose

rubble of the sidehill. For a moment they stood surveying the wreckage of the cat-train. The cat lay overturned against a jutting pinnacle of rock. The wagons were mere jumbles of splintered wood at the edge of the green timber below. Scott felt his hopes fading.

But the policeman observed, "It could have been worse. These cats are rugged machines. They can take a lot of punishment. The pipe has fetched up among the trees, instead of rolling into the river, and the top-load of case goods and sacks seems to be still inside the tarps. You'll be able to salvage most of it. I think Tim will have new wagons on the trail in three weeks or so."

Three weeks! His father needed that pipe right now! Scott stared dully at what was left of the wagons. One rear axle stood on end, the wheels still intact. Queer how they had escaped being smashed—a little creepy the way the wheel poised in the air seemed to be still turning. Three weeks! Half the summer would be gone. What would happen to the mine?

The constable broke into Scott's thoughts. "Well, let's get hold of that rope."

The boy scrambled down and tugged at a rope's end that protruded from the wreckage. He recognized it as the brake-rope of the rear wagon. Coiling it up hand over hand, he gave a sharp jerk and the broken end whipped toward him.

For a second or two he gazed at it. Queer! His mind seemed to be spinning slowly—like the wheel on the up-ended axle. Were his eyes playing him tricks? He touched the end of the rope. Suddenly he was shouting, "Constable

Black! Look at this!"

Scott held the rope out to the constable. "Look!" His voice shook with excitement. "Only the outside fibers are frayed! See! The inside strands are smooth. They look as though they'd been cut with a knife!"

The constable picked up the rope as though he were handling a poisonous snake. "By ginger! I'd been wondering—Tim rigs new rope every season—and it takes more beef than you and Jimmy Brokenose have to snap half-inch manila."

"I don't understand." Scott's brain still seemed to be going around in circles. "How could anyone cut the inside of the strands without it showing from the outside?" He picked up a bight of the rope and twisted the strands back against the lay, parting them as one does when preparing to make a splice. "I suppose it could be done. My knife would be too big . . . but a small double-edged blade, with a sharp point, would do the trick, wouldn't it?"

"That's one way it could be done, I suppose," the constable replied guardedly. He cut off about a foot from the end of the rope and then located the short piece that still remained on the brake lever. He wrapped the two pieces in canvas and stowed them in one of the big pockets in his tunic.

"Why?" The sinister implications of his discovery seemed to hold Scott's mind tangled like a fly in a spider web. "Why should anyone do such a thing?"

"That's what we'll have to find out." Constable Black gave him a dead-pan look. "Can you think of anyone who was out to get you?"

Scott grinned wryly. "Gosh, no! I'm not that important." Then his face clouded. "How about Bunny . . . you don't suppose . . ."

It was the policeman's turn to smile. "I wouldn't be surprised to hear of somebody punching that young hothead in the jaw. But nobody would try to kill him." He shook his head in puzzlement. "Nobody would want to hold up the freight. The mine is a good thing for everybody. It means a chance for the trappers to earn money in the summer—more business for the freighters and traders."

Scott blurted out, "How about Jimmy Brokenose? He told me his grandfather was a chief and his name had something to do with fighting. Jim didn't seem to want to talk about his family. Do you suppose he has enemies?"

"I don't know about Jimmy." Constable Black looked thoughtful. "These northern tribes were never warlike. However, there was bloodshed sometimes, when their hunting grounds bordered those of the southern tribes. A small party of Tahltans might come on two or three of the Naas River hunters and kill them. It was a life for a life in those days and the feud might go on for generations."

Scott remained silent. Could that be the reason why Jim hadn't wanted to talk about his ancestors? An old inter-tribal blood feud? Jim was the grandson of a chief —he might always be in vague fear for his life.

The policeman went on meditatively. "Wrecking a cat-train to try to kill Jimmy Brokenose doesn't seem like an Indian's way of evening up an old score. A rifle shot up in the mountains would be more like the way they'd settle things. However, I'll have to look into the question of these old Indian feuds. That and your idea about a small, double-edged knife, with a sharp point, are about all we have to go on."

It was on the tip of Scott's tongue to add, "And the Jack o' Diamonds Claim on Magpie Creek." But he choked the words back, remembering Captain Dan's warning to keep them secret.

Later, as the two were climbing back to the ledge, the constable's tone was brusque as he warned Scott. "Not a word about this to anyone. There'll be enough rumors carried by moccasin telegraph as it is. This is the most mysterious affair I've ever come across."

Another secret to lock in his mind! Scott felt a wave of loneliness surge through him at the thought that he had no one to share the burden with him. Then, as they arrived on the ledge, he shrugged the feeling off at the sound of Bunny's voice calling to him.

"Just wanted to say I didn't mean anything by the way I razzed you. I guess I got into the way of pretending I was tough. You see, I was the youngest of five kids and we never had much of anything, even before the drought hit the farm. I was out on my own before I finished grade eight and it seemed like I had to fight for everything I got. You understand, don't you?"

"Sure, I know how it goes." Scott thought he could be forgiven the implied white lie, for he had spoken as if he really had known all along what it was like to leave school so young and have to fight for everything one got.

The cat-skinner went on. "Guys called me Bunny because they said I had long ears . . ." He broke off at the sound of footsteps returning to the ledge.

Scott followed close beside the stretcher as the men inched it up the rocks and then trudged along the road to the pickup truck at the top of the hill. They lifted Bunny into the back of the pickup and the starter whirred. Scott reached for the hand of Bunny's uninjured arm. They were saying good-bye with a left handshake—he wished he had time to tell Bunny about the Scout's handshake.

His patient said, "I don't know how to thank you for what you've done."

Scott whispered, "You shouldn't let people kid you. I've seen lots of rabbits with ears longer than yours."

The grind of the truck's gears drowned out Bunny's reply. But for Scott it was sufficient to see an impudent grin spread across the freckled face. It conveyed far more than any words Bunny might have spoken.

The pickup swayed and sideslipped as it crawled in low gear along the muddy ruts and disappeared among the trees. The doctor was sitting in the back, doing what he could to keep the stretcher from sliding around. Even so, Scott realized that Bunny would suffer stabbing pain before the jolting ride was over. Would he keep smiling? Somehow Scott felt he would.

Tim said, "Now we'll get to work. Figure the best place to set up camp will be in the trees, just below the wreckage. Jim, you and Scott carry my bed-roll and this box of grub. I'll look after my tool box."

Down in the canyon, Tim observed, "Sure was lucky! I caught Gee-gee before he started out with the telegraph line supplies. He should be here with his pack-string in a couple of days."

A couple of days! Then perhaps . . . "Will there be enough horses to take all the pipe in one trip?" Scott demanded.

"Pipe?" Tim kept his eyes riveted on the canvas lean-to he was lashing up. "They'll take the boxes and gunnies—I guess those lengths of pipe are too long and too heavy to pack on a horse."

The answer left Scott numb. Tim glanced at him. "Sure, at least Gee-gee's horses will be some use to us. But that long face you're pulling will be no help at all."

Scott tried to brighten up as he turned to the jobs at hand. But he could not keep thoughts of his father from crowding into his mind. Scott could picture him all too clearly, worried and anxious as he awaited the arrival of the freight.

That afternoon, and for the next two days in the canyon, Scott tried to keep working so he would have little time to worry about the future. There seemed to be a peculiar satisfaction in the salvage work. Each broken box presented a new problem as to how it should be repaired. It was good to sweat at the job of collecting the scattered lengths of pipe and stacking them in an orderly pile. And it was some consolation to discover that, apart from a few dents, the pipe had escaped damage. After the hard work was done, it seemed relaxing, under Tim's supervision, to help blaze a trail from their camp to meet the road, at a point just above where the bridge crossed the river.

Scott's worries didn't affect his appetite and he couldn't remember ever before enjoying food as much as he did the bacon and beans that Tim cooked over the open campfire. The nights under the canvas lean-to were something to look back on, too, for he could lie in his sleeping bag and look up at the moon-lit clouds floating across the treetops.

On the third night, the sky had cleared and Scott lay awake staring up at the stars. He was restless and felt a new uneasiness, for Gee-gee's pack-train should have arrived by now. Tim and Jimmy Brokenose had given Scott little comfort with their stories about the difficulties involved in keeping a big pack-string together—especially at the start of a trip.

"Ornery critters!" Tim remarked. "Probably they all headed back for town last night."

Scott tried to tell himself that there was nothing more he could do about the freight. Go to sleep and forget about it! Odd how the stars seem closer when you're down in a canyon. . . . Stars seem to make you feel nothing is impossible—not even loading hydraulic pipe on pack horses.

The letter in Scott's pocket was clear proof that his father had expected his son to arrange to get the pipe in, no matter what happened. "Be tactful," it said—but tact could hardly help now. Or could it?

Scott's thoughts wandered back to the previous summer. Like most boys of his age, he was never enthusiastic about mowing lawns. He remembered his father saying, before he left for the mine, "It's a pity you're not a year older—then I wouldn't have to pay a man to cut the grass while I'm away." Scott had demonstrated that he was not too young for the job.

Something like that might work with Gee-gee. Scott had an idea that the old man's pack-train could handle the pipe, if Gee-gee went to a little extra trouble. "By Golly!" Scott thought. "I'll try it . . . tact . . . tact and a little diplomacy. It may work!"

He snuggled down into his robe and was soon asleep.

Next morning, the boy didn't have long to wait before he had a chance to try out his idea. Shortly before ten o'clock, the campers heard the thud of hoofs on the trail they had blazed beside the river. "*Hi-yup! Hi-yipe-ee!*" Scott heard the shouts of the Indian wranglers growing louder. Suddenly, horses were snorting and whinnying all around him as they shied away from the camp.

"There must be some way to load that pipe," Scott told himself as he looked at the unused lash ropes coiled around the wood "saw-bucks" of the empty packsaddles. Keeping a wary eye on the stamping hoofs, he made his way through the milling animals toward the spot where Gee-gee had reined in his pinto mare.

"Hi-ya, Scott!" The boy couldn't quite understand the change in Gee-gee's appearance. On foot he was just a little, gray-haired, old man—in the saddle, well, he looked as though he belonged there.

"Hear you fellows have some freight for us to pick up," he remarked casually.

Scott thought: I haven't a chance with my diplomacy! But I'll try it anyway. "Sure thing!" he answered. "Those boxes and sacks are all ready for you. We've stacked the pipe over there, out of your way. It'll have to wait until the cat is running again—I know you can't take it."

Gee-gee's jaw worked rapidly but no words seemed to come out. His beard wigwagged for several seconds before he spoke. "Can't pack pipe over the trail? Who in Tophet told you that?"

Scott shrugged. "I don't know . . . I just thought. Won't the horses shy at carrying anything that long?"

"Thunderation! Lad, you've another think coming. 'Tain't no freight goes over this trail that my horses can't handle."

Gee-gee bellowed to his packer and the two wranglers. "Leave the young stock to pack these groceries. Round up the best horses to load the pipe. It won't be hard to handle. We'll put blinders on the critters and there'll be two of us on each side to do the lifting."

The pinto mare wheeled and trotted off toward the pipe as though she could read Gee-gee's mind. Scott saw Tim sauntering across to him, surprise lighting up his gray eyes. "Didn't hear what you told him, but you must have a head on your shoulders to think up a way of persuading Gee-gee to handle cargo like that pipe."

Scott just looked up at him and grinned.

10

SCOTT RIDES THE CASSIAR TRAIL

The pack horses clattered over a wooden bridge to the north bank of the Tuya and plodded up a steep hill. Gee-gee had saddled a cobby sorrel, called Mac, for Scott, and the boy's teeth rattled with the animal's ponderous trot that jarred his spine. Still, Scott was proud of the jaunty way he'd waved good-bye to Tim and Jimmy Brokenose.

"Don't worry," Tim called after him. "We've lots of time to get this cat running before the new wagons are shipped up-river."

Jim reminded him, "Don't forget to tell my folks I said they must give you some real number one moose steaks. You'll probably stop overnight near their camp."

Halfway up the hill, Scott didn't feel so sure of himself as when he waved farewell. His mount slowed down to a walk. Mac's body appeared to move in four directions at once. The saddle seemed wide enough to fit an elephant. Scott decided to dismount and lead his horse to the top of the hill.

Gee-gee, swaying easily with every movement of the pinto, rode up close behind. "You're liable to blister your heels, walking up a hill like this," the old man commented with a guffaw.

Scott smiled, in spite of his discomfort. "It's not my heels I'm worrying about. I want to be able to sit around the campfire tonight like a real wrangler." Within the next four days, he told himself, he was going to learn to let his body swing in the saddle in tune with Mac's gait. And he was going to learn something else, too; how to throw the diamond-hitch next time they lashed the camp gear on the old pack horse called Oscar.

Gee-gee had made old Oscar Scott's special charge, and Oscar presented a challenge. He knew all the tricks. He held his wind while his cinch was being tightened, in hopes that later, when he deflated, he would be able to work his pack loose. And, if he was discouraged by a sharp jab in the ribs from the packer's knee, he would patiently bide his time, hoping that his attempts to rub his pack off against a tree would go unnoticed.

At the top of the long hill, Scott stiffly climbed into the saddle again. He knew there were mountains in the distance, hidden in the mist, but the sun was shining through the clouds over a rolling plateau country. The land was sparsely covered with pine and spruce and clumps of white mountain birch dotted the nearer hillsides, among the light green blanket of aspens. Wild roses brightened the hollows with pink and the trail ahead was lined with delphinium and fireweed. Between the borders of blue and magenta, the line of bobbing packs were strung out as far ahead as Scott could see.

Later, when the sun blinked through the trees to bar the trail with long shadows, the wranglers started to herd the pack-string into a clearing. Mac covered the last hundred yards at a loping gallop. Scott waved his hat in the air and shouted, "Yipee!" as the ground streaked by below him. But, when they neared the campsite, Mac abruptly slowed to a jolting trot. Scott clutched wildly for the saddle horn, one foot slipped out of the stirrup and he found himself sitting on the ground.

No one appeared to have witnessed his undignified arrival. For this, he was very thankful. I'll do better tomorrow, Scott told himself grimly as he got up and looked around to locate Gee-gee.

The old man was standing with his back to Scott, waving to a group of Indian women and children at a small encampment across the clearing. "Jimmy's mother and her sister," Gee-gee explained as he turned to Scott. "Jim thought they'd be camped here. I guess his father, Tom Brokenose, and the other hunter are out after fresh meat."

The Indians were busy shooing the horses away from their camp as the wranglers turned them loose after unloading their packs. Mingled with their shrill voices, Scott was aware of the continuous barking of a very excited little dog.

He caught occasional glimpses of the animal as it flashed back and forth among the trees on straight, slender legs. It was coal black, except for white boots and a white patch on one side of its chest. Its long, slender muzzle and rather wide, pricked ears reminded Scott of a fox, but its short, bushy tail that pointed straight up like a huge shaving brush was quite different from that of any other animal he could recall.

"Tahltan bear dog," Gee-gee boomed. "I'll unsaddle Mac—you go over and have a look at him."

Scott strolled over to the Indian camp, whistling softly and snapping his fingers. The dog held his ground until he was within twenty feet and then vanished like a ghost among the aspens, but a new barrage of shrill yelps told that he was not far away.

One of the Indian women smiled at Scott. "Crazy little dog! He's just a pup. Keep still—we call him back."

She coaxed softly in her own language and the bear dog suddenly appeared in the space between the tents. He eyed Scott warily, but little by little he edged toward him. Scott remained motionless until the dog was close enough to sniff nervously at his hand. But when he attempted to pat its head, it exploded into a flash of black and white fur. Seconds later, a volley of yaps directly behind him made Scott turn so quickly that he was thrown completely off balance.

The woman rocked with laughter. "He fool you, just the same he fool bear. Move around so fast you get all mixed up."

Suddenly the dog lost interest in the boy and wheeled around to stand looking up the trail, quivering from head to tail. Scott's eyes, drawn in the same direction, caught sight of the returning hunters plodding homeward. Their rifles were slung over their shoulders and behind them waddled three big sled dogs with bloodstained packs on their backs.

The little dog uttered a pleased whimper and bounded over to meet them. He streaked in among the pack dogs like a flash of lightning. Then, almost as quickly as a thunderbolt, an avalanche of furry bodies and snapping jaws engulfed him.

Scott's heart pounded in his breast as he ran toward them. The hunters, with a few hard kicks and jabs of their rifle butts, stopped the fight almost as quickly as it started. By the time the boy arrived, the pack dogs were plodding stolidly on toward the tents. Behind them, huddled in a patch of lupine by the roadside, lay a little bundle of black and white fur.

Awed by the brief flare-up of savagery he had just witnessed, Scott knelt down beside the limp figure. His hand touched a nose that was wet and cold. Somewhere beneath the white patch of fur, now stained crimson with blood, he could feel the bear dog's rapid heartbeat.

He heard the gruff voice of one of the hunters behind him. "That fool little dog—he never learn sense. Guess he's done for now!"

The boy protested. "No! No! His heart's still beating. Perhaps he's more scared than hurt."

The Indian shrugged his chunky shoulders. "Maybe— maybe you fix'um up. Wranglers tell me my son Jimmy says you're good medicine man. You fix cat-skinner— maybe you fix dog."

"I'll try." Scott gathered the dog up in his arms. He was far from confident. As he walked toward the wranglers' campfire, he was thinking how difficult it would be to nurse an animal who couldn't tell you where it was hurt.

Nobody paid much attention as he laid the dog down in the shelter of his dunnage. Gee-gee was sympathetic but he made no pretense of feeling there was any hope. "Happens all the time. Seems like the work-dogs are jealous of these little tikes—and once one of them gets chewed up, there's not much you can do for it."

Then, apparently noticing the trembling of Scott's lips, he spoke gently. "Don't take it too hard. He's not your dog. Supper's ready. You'll feel better after you get some of that moose-meat inside you."

The meat was indeed something to be thankful for after a long day on the trail, but Scott hurried through his meal in silence. He took a few tender scraps over to the dog, but it only raised its head to sniff at them and made no attempt to eat.

However, the dog had at least licked at the food. This gave Scott an idea. He went back to the fire and picked up a marrowbone that had been set aside for the work-dogs. He put it in a pot of water and hung it over the fire to simmer.

He boiled another kettle of water and dissolved a little salt in it. After it cooled, he went over to sponge the dog's wounds. He noted, with a faint flicker of hope, that it turned its head toward him as he approached.

The dog lay passive as he stroked its body. As far as he could tell, there were no broken bones—just two deep gashes, one across the back and another across the right flank. But they had stopped bleeding and they were both in places where the dog could lick them clean.

Scott fetched a dish of the broth, dipped his finger in it and let the dog lick it off. Then he held the dish under its muzzle and its pink tongue reached out and slowly lapped up the contents.

The boy looked up and saw Jim's father coming over from the Indian camp. Scott rose to meet him and, as he moved, the dog whimpered, raised himself on his forelegs and made a feeble attempt to crawl after him.

The Indian looked at Scott with approval. "That little dog likes you. You want him? You take him with you—huh?"

Scott hesitated. Did the Indian really want him to keep the dog? It seemed too good to be true!

"Go on—you keep him," Tom urged. "You make good medicine. I want you take this dog—bye and bye and you make him skookum again."

"Wow! Thanks a million, Tom. I'll take good care of him—I know he'll get better." Scott fondled the dog's ears and noticed his beady black eyes look up appealingly. Gee-gee stamped up behind them.

"Thunderation! You've taken on a pack of trouble. Like as not that slash on his hindquarters has hamstrung him and he'll always be lame. How's he going to get over the trail, if he can't walk?"

Gee-gee's beard added an exclamation mark after the question. But Scott's jaw set stubbornly. "He's going to get better—I know he is. I'll fix a place for him to ride on Oscar's top-pack."

"The way you're going about it, I guess he might have a chance to get better." Gee-gee hesitated. "Sure—you could wrap him in a manty and put him on Oscar. What's his name?"

Tom answered with a word that sounded to Scott like a combined cough and a sneeze. It would have to be something simpler than that, the boy decided. He looked at Gee-gee. "What was that you said I could wrap him in?"

"A manty. Thought you'd know by now that a manty is the canvas cover we put over a pack."

"That's his name from now on." Scott sat down and stroked the dog's glossy fur. "Manty! Hullo, Manty boy! Manty! Manty!" The bear dog's ears twitched as though he liked the sound of his new name.

Early the next morning the camp was girdled with a wreath of wood smoke and the fragrance of coffee and bacon lingered after breakfast, to mingle with the smell of horseflesh and saddle leather.

Scott hoisted a bundle of dunnage and held it against Oscar's packsaddle while Gee-gee, from the other side, flipped the lash-rope to him. Under—over—over . . . they passed the rope back and forth and then Scott tied the final knot to complete the diamond-hitch.

"How's that? Can I throw a diamond-hitch or can't I?"

Gee-gee nodded. "You catch on fast!"

Scott stepped back to survey the pack. He was learning to pull his own weight with the rest of the pack-train crew.

The pipe was loaded, ready to start on another day's journey northward. In high spirits, Scott stooped to pick up Manty. Carefully, he set him on the top-pack and drew the canvas snugly over him so that just his head was showing. Manty's eyes were bright as they watched Scott swing into the saddle.

The boy said to himself, "I'm sure he's going to get better now—I can tell by the way he looks at me. Maybe he'll be a bit lame—what of it? He's a one-man dog—and I'll be his man."

Scott rode close beside old Oscar for the rest of the trip so he could keep an eye on Manty. The first day was clear, with blistering sunshine, but at night it cooled off quickly and there was a thin skim of ice on the water bucket in the morning. Next day, as they left the valley of the Stikine and climbed gradually up toward the divide, dark rain clouds rolled in from the west.

Hail and icy raindrops pelted the pack-train and the horses floundered in sticky mud. In places, deep wagon ruts forced them to detour through the trees to prevent the horses from being mired down.

Gee-gee reined in beside Scott. "Blasted wagons! That's what's ruined this trail!" The boy was startled by the note of bitterness in the old man's voice. He glanced uneasily at the way Gee-gee clutched the ivory butt of a big revolver in his holster. The wrangler had boasted how he could shoot the head off a spruce hen at twenty paces with that gun. Now he looked as though he would like to use it to blast the cat-train off the trail.

The old man noticed Scott's startled look and chuckled. "Feel more at home with Old Betsy along. Have to keep her out of sight while I'm in town. This country is getting too high-toned. Oh well! Guess I haven't got a very good name with the police, anyway."

Scott turned his eyes away from Gee-gee and stared self-consciously at Manty's head, peeking out from the top-pack. The boy suddenly remembered how Gee-gee had disappeared from Tim's cabin when the constable stopped by. And now Gee-gee said he was in the bad books of the police! He thought of the constable, at the scene of the wreck, saying, "Everybody wants the mine to go ahead —it means more business for the freighters." Which freighters? Business had come to Gee-gee because the cat had been wrecked.

It was all very confusing, Scott felt. Gee-gee hated the cat-train. Did he also have it in for the mine which had its freight hauled in by the wagons?

Somebody must have had a reason for cutting the brake-rope. Surely, Gee-gee couldn't be the guilty one. Why, he had plunged into the grizzly infested swamps at the Boundary to come to the aid of Scott and Jack. . . .

"Hi! Hup! Gee over a bit, Oscar!"

It was wet and cold riding through the rain-drenched brush. Scott shivered for a moment. He didn't want to think about the wreck. He didn't want to think about Gee-gee and his revolver. He didn't want to wonder about his missing rock samples. He wanted only to keep Manty in sight and to dream of the days soon coming, when, with nothing to worry about, he and his dog would go for long hikes together.

11

ON THE FRINGE OF THE
CASSIAR RANGE

A T noon of his fourth day in the saddle, Scott hardly noticed the change in Mac's gait as the horse splashed through a shallow stream cutting across the trail. Walk, trot or canter—it was all the same to Scott now. He swayed easily in the saddle with the rhythm of every change in pace.

It was all downhill from here on. Mac broke into a brisk trot. Scott said to himself, "I've got this problem licked—even if I do seem to bump around in the saddle a bit more than Gee-gee does."

Gee-gee seemed to be floating along beside him. "That was One Mile Creek—we're nearly there!" he shouted.

Scott shot a sideways glance at the old man. Gee-gee seemed as excited as a child to be nearing the end of their journey. Nothing had happened during the last two days on the trail to give Scott any clue as to why Gee-gee should have a bad record with the police. Surely it couldn't be as a gunman—Gee-gee had tried three times to "shoot the head off a spruce hen at twenty paces"—and he had missed completely! Scott couldn't bring himself to believe that the wrangler had cut the brake-rope. But Gee-gee had been the only one to gain anything by the wreck . . . it was hard to forget that.

"There she is!"

Scott caught his breath at the sight of the silvery-blue surface of Dease Lake, shimmering below them. Less than a mile in width, its waters stretched northward to a narrow strait between a massive, round-topped mountain on the west and dark, spruce-clad hills on the opposite shore. Far in the distance, white peaks made a jagged line across the northern horizon. The Cassiar Range!

"Osprey Creek heads somewhere among those peaks," Scott thought. He lowered his eyes and saw a sheet-iron warehouse at the lakeshore. Two men had just come out of it and were walking up toward them. As they drew near, he saw that one was a dark, hairy giant of a man and the other was a tall, slender, olive-skinned youth.

"Here come Antoin and his son, Pierre," Gee-gee said, reining in his pinto mare at the edge of a clearing about a hundred yards from the water. Behind them, the pack horses were flowing down the hill like a river. One of Gee-gee's wranglers had already dismounted and was preparing to set up camp at a site marked by bare tent poles, a few yards from Antoin's cabin.

Antoin strode up and gripped the saddle horn of Gee-gee's pinto. "What's this?" he bellowed. "Ver' best stage of water on the river. One whole week we have the boat tied up. Every day we listen for the cat-train. Now! What happens? No wagons—just horses! Bah!"

"Accident—the outfit jackknifed on Tuya Hill," Gee-gee explained briefly.

Scott dismounted and lifted Manty to the ground. The dog limped close at his heels as he strode over to Antoin. The boy had made up his mind he ought to let Antoin know right away that the pipe had to be given precedence over any other freight.

"I'm Scott Haliburton."

"Of course! M'sieu Haliburton's son. Welcome to the Lake." The big man's handshake felt as though a little more pressure might have broken every bone in Scott's hand. "Now—you must excuse us. We are in a big hurry to load the boat."

"That's what I wanted to talk to you about." Scott's words came easily because he had spent all morning going over them in his mind. "We have a load of pipe here that has to get to the mine before anything else does."

Antoin waved his hands. "Next trip—next trip we take the pipe. We already have some groceries in the boat—to unload them would be crazy!"

Suzette, Antoin's wife, appeared on the porch of the cabin overlooking the lake. "Kettle's boiling! I know you men—you will want tea before you start to work."

Scott shot a casual glance at the speaker. A black cat was clawing playfully at the hem of her bright print dress. Scott had no time to look at cats. He had business to settle and he didn't welcome the interruption. He looked up at Antoin in deadly earnest.

"If you have other freight in the boat, it will have to

be unloaded. The pipe definitely has to go this trip."

"*Yipe!*"

Scott spun around.

"*Yipe! Yipe!*"

Manty was bounding toward the cabin on all four legs. Golly! There didn't seem to be anything wrong with him now. Manty hardly seemed to limp as he circled the front steps.

The cat crouched on the porch with its fur fluffed up and its tail lashing. It held its ground, hissing and spitting defiance as Manty hopped up the steps with his teeth bared.

"Manty! Stop! Come back here!" Scott yelled.

Antoin snatched him by the shoulder and jerked him around. "So! He is your dog! But when you call he does not obey!"

"But . . . he was hurt. He . . ."

"Dogs!" Antoin seemed to spit out the word. "If he hurts Bête-noir, your freight can wait. I will take the trade goods down to Liard Post first!"

The barking had stopped. Scott wished the riverman would let go of his shoulder. He wanted to see what was happening. He wondered why Gee-gee looked so amused.

"Hold your hosses, Antoin!" The old man guffawed. "Bête-noir doesn't seem to need any help."

Antoin relaxed his grip and Scott was able to turn toward the cabin. There was Manty, stretched out on the porch with his tail wagging furiously. The cat was stepping daintily back and forth in front of him, fur smooth and unruffled now. Every once and a while the two animals touched noses and Manty's tail wagged harder than ever.

Antoin's bushy eyebrows arched up. "They are friends! But we are all friends, are we not? Come, young Haliburton—first we drink tea and then we load this pipe of yours."

Scott didn't need a second invitation. He'd had nothing to eat since breakfast. The mulligan that Suzette set before him called for a second—and then a third helping. But it wasn't so much the food or the scalding tea that sent a warm glow through his body. It was the realization that the last worry about shipment of the pipe was over. It would be at Osprey Creek by tomorrow evening.

Scott had never seen such a boat as Antoin's. It was flat-bottomed and had a wide, square stern that contrasted oddly with the graceful flare of the straight-stemmed bow. It had no deck and seemed only a little larger than the big lifeboats carried by the coastal steamers. It took all afternoon to unload the groceries from the boat and to trundle the pipe along a narrow log float and stow it aboard.

Once the work started, Antoin opened his mouth only to grunt an occasional word of instruction to Pierre or Scott. The two rivermen set a pace that Scott found it hard to maintain. However, by the time the big tarps were lashed over the cargo, he felt satisfied that he had done his share.

As he trudged up to the pack-train camp, he was surprised by the sight of two mounted men, followed by two pack horses, jogging down the trail. Gee-gee, standing by the campfire, wagged his head at him with approval. "Kept my boys on the jump, feeding that pipe to you. You fellows sure rolled her onboard in a hurry!"

Scott pointed up the trail. "Look! Who in heck is that?"

The old man wheeled around and squinted into the sun. "It's that dude, Gold Brick! He couldn't have been far behind us."

The two men dismounted between the pack-train camp and the cabin. Scott and Gee-gee walked over to meet them. Gold Brick, after a brief, "Hi, there Scotty!" drew Gee-gee off to one side. Scott was left alone with the other man—a square-faced, unsmiling Indian.

"Hi! Have a good trip?" Scott asked.

He tried to sound genuinely interested. But more than half his mind was with Gold Brick and Gee-gee. What were they talking about?

The Indian scowled. "Maybe," he mumbled. Abruptly he turned away from Scott and began unloading the camp gear from the pack horses. From his manner, it didn't appear likely that he would welcome any offer of assistance. Scott stood and watched him for several minutes until Gee-gee and Gold Brick sauntered back.

"Come on—time for chow." Gee-gee dismissed Gold Brick with a nod and beckoned to Scott. When he was sure they were out of earshot, Scott said quietly, "Gosh! That Indian sure doesn't talk much. His face reminds me of those totem poles at Wrangell."

Gee-gee chuckled. "That's Tommy Naas. He's sort of a lone wolf. Doesn't rightly belong in these parts. His people live to the south of the Tahltans—in the old days they were always feudin' with each other."

Scott ate his supper in silence, staring thoughtfully into the fire. Indian bloodfeuds? Tommy's tribesmen were ancient enemies of the Tahltans. And Jimmy Brokenose was the grandson of a Tahltan chief. Was that the key to the wrecked wagons?

Scott looked around at Tommy, silhouetted against the fire at Gold Brick's camp, a few yards uphill. He could make out a small sheath knife at the Indian's belt. Was it a double-edged knife with a sharp point? From this angle, Tommy's square face seemed to be set in the middle of his chunky shoulders as though he had no neck. Why did it look so familiar? Suddenly Scott thought he knew why. He was almost certain now that he had glimpsed the reflection of a face like that, mirrored in the water tank at Telegraph Creek!

Scott finished his dinner and then strolled over toward Antoin's cabin. The door stood open and, from the sound of voices inside, it was evident that a regular gab-fest was in progress. Antoin and Gold Brick were both going "great guns" about the accident at the Tuya. As the only on-the-spot witness, Scott expected to be consulted. It soon dawned on him, however, that the two men preferred their own vivid imaginations to any information he had to offer. He was annoyed for a moment, then amused, and finally, bored. With a snap of his fingers to Manty, he slipped out of the cabin, made his way to his mosquito tent and turned in. It had been a strenuous day. He was tired and sleepy.

"*Woof!*"

Scott was snapped out of a deep, dreamless sleep. There was just enough light in the tent for him to see Manty standing with his neck-ruff up, like the quills of a porcupine. He hissed at the dog to be quiet and cautiously lifted a corner of the netting to try and see what had alarmed him.

It must have been well after midnight. There was no sign of a light in the tents or the cabin, but there was enough pre-dawn grayness in the eastern sky for Scott to make out the figure of Gold Brick, walking up from the lake. Manty jumped out in front of his master and snarled.

"Something wrong?" There was note of mockery in Gold Brick's voice.

"M-Manty woke me up." Surprise made Scott stammer.

"You'll get used to that. Those Indian pooches will bark at their own shadow. I was just fetching a bucket of water for the morning." Gold Brick half-raised his right arm in proof of the last statement.

"Oh . . . I see."

Scott was glad to get out of the chill air and back into his sleeping bag. His watch said it was ten minutes to two. A queer time to be getting water for breakfast. Had Gold Brick and Antoin been talking all night? Could be, Scott thought and slipped off to sleep.

He awoke to the sound of Antoin bellowing, "Scott! Pierre! Hurry! It is flat-calm on the lake. We must cross before the wind gets up!"

When the boy arrived at the landing, Pierre was clamping two big outboards on the transom. His dark eyes glowed with pride as he told Scott, "These are the new twenty-four horse models."

Scott was impressed. They were the biggest kickers he

had ever seen.

Antoin explained with gusto, "I don't steer by the little handle on the kickers. That is all right for picnics on the lake but on the river you need the long sweep to turn quickly. And I don't stop every hour to fill the little tanks. I have one big tank in the stern. Yesterday I filled it up —now we forget about gas until we are home again."

Pierre pushed the boat away from the shore with a long pike-pole. Antoin whipped back one starting cord and then the other. The big kickers purred like twin tigers. Antoin stood up in the stern. One hand on the steering-sweep was all he needed to keep the boat headed due north.

Scott and Pierre made themselves comfortable amongst the dunnage in the bow and Manty stood with his fore-paws on the gunnel. They drew near to a pair of loons, paddling slowly across their bow. The dog's tail twitched with excitement. Both boys roared with laughter at Manty's puzzled expression when the birds arched their long necks and dived out of sight.

After that, there wasn't much to watch except the waves fanning out from the bow across the smooth, silver surface; spreading in an ever widening vee until they reached along the shores and made the hills curtsy to the boat as it passed. Scott felt he might have fallen asleep, were it not for the chill in the morning air.

Two hours later, the lake was behind them and they could feel the warmth of the nooning sun. Now the boat responded to the first gentle tug of the current of the Dease River. Thick clusters of willows overhung the narrow channel and marshy flats beyond marked the mouth of a tributary creek. The rugged shape of the Cassiar Range was drawing always nearer on the horizon.

Pierre settled back against the dunnage. "Pretty soft! Hey?"

Scott felt a chill creep over him. Strange, he thought, only a couple of minutes ago I was thinking of peeling off my jacket. Then he remembered: "Pretty soft!" Those were the words Jimmy Brokenose had used at the start of the trip over the trail. Pierre's unconscious repetition of them had struck a jarring note in Scott's mind.

He glanced back at Antoin, standing confidently at the steering-sweep. He looked ahead at the milky water, with hardly a ripple creasing its surface.

Scott grinned. Superstitious, he thought with a shrug, as superstitious as Captain Dan! There was nothing to worry about. Compared with the Stikine, the Dease could hardly be called a river.

12

WRECKED IN THE RAPIDS

Swollen by the water of creeks tumbling down from melting snow fields, the Dease began to look more like a real river to Scott as the boat glided downstream into the heart of the Cassiar Mountains. But the channel was still narrow and Antoin had to steer carefully to avoid the "sweepers"—uprooted trees that reached out from the bank ahead of them. Pierre no longer lolled against the dunnage, but stood now, ever alert, with the pike-pole in his hands.

Bare mountain peaks came into view and disappeared as the channel took the boat under the shadow of the forests.

Scott said, "There's one big, flat-topped peak—sometimes it's ahead of us—sometimes astern. But every time we see the mountains, I can pick it out."

Pierre didn't take his eyes off the channel. "That's Anvil Mountain. The river's pretty crooked here. But, by and by, that mountain will always be ahead. It's right across the river from Osprey Creek."

A pair of great brown fish hawks with white breasts, perched on a tall tree, paid no attention to the boat as it droned beneath them.

"Ospreys?" Scott asked.

Pierre glanced up quickly and smiled. "That's right! At the rate we're going, we'll be at Osprey Creek in about four hours."

At midday, Antoin steered the boat in to a gravel bar. A bull moose, his dark bulk blending with the shadows of the forest, stood motionless in the water as they approached. As soon as the engines stopped, the big animal picked up his long legs, splashed through the shallows, and disappeared into the woods.

Scott's ears were ringing from the drone of the kickers. The lapping of the river against the gravel came to him only as a sort of tinkle, but he could vaguely sense a steady, dull roar. Whether it was a buzzing inside his head, or whether it came from a distance, he couldn't be sure. From the stern, Antoin's voice sounded blurred and far away.

"Good! A fine place for lunch. On this bar we have lots of dry driftwood and no mosquitoes. In the woods, the mosquitoes would eat us alive!"

They built a fire and had the kettle boiling while the hoofprints of the moose still showed wet in the gravel. Pierre produced bread and cheese and cold roast moose meat from the grub box. Nobody spoke for the next few minutes until, suddenly, Antoin angrily slapped at his cheek. *"Zut!* The mosquitoes have found us—no matter —we have nearly finished. Soon we will shoot the rapids

—after that—three hours and we will be at Osprey Creek."

The rapids! Scott realized the source of the dull roar in his ears.

Antoin finished his tea with a loud, gurgling sound and made his way to the stern of the boat. His bushy eyebrows knit in a frown. He glared at the engines. "Pierre! You understand these hoopen-annies. Is it time to turn on the big gas tank?"

Pierre hurried to his father. He spoke eagerly. "Yes! See—the gauge says the feed tank is nearly empty. Turn this valve now and the gas will run in from the big tank."

Scott jumped into the boat and helped to push the bow away from the shore. Antoin started the kickers and the boat glided smoothly downstream for half an hour. Then they rounded a sharp bend in the river.

"Watch this!" Pierre muttered without turning. "White water, here we come!"

Scott gasped as he saw how the stream had narrowed. The entire channel between the dark green spruce along the banks was a mass of white foam, surging amongst huge, rounded boulders. "Wow!" he exclaimed. "How do we get through that?"

Pierre jerked his head toward the stern. Scott glanced back and saw Antoin grasping the steering-sweep with both hands. Then the boy looked ahead with confidence. Antoin would steer them through!

The current caught hold of the boat and it suddenly shot ahead toward a white ridge of ragged water that danced along the center of the channel. The bow veered away from the foaming crest in midstream—straight for a huge boulder on the left bank. Then, just as it seemed the boat was going to crash headlong on to the rocks, she sheared off, surging up over the dark green swell that curled back from the boulder. She slid down into the trough and spray shot up from the bow as she pounded into the combers ahead. Pitching and lurching, she broke through the white ridge of foam and headed for the opposite bank.

Antoin moved the sweep back and forth so they headed along the center of a trough, where white water folded back between two boulders. Pierre stood rigid at the bow, with the pike-pole clutched in both hands. Scott, crouched just behind him, one hand on Manty, who was peering over the bow. A huge swell reared up and towered along beside them for a matter of seconds. Then it vanished and the boat darted away from it.

Scott half-rose to his feet. Scarcely more than a hundred yards ahead, he could see smooth water where the over-hanging willows barely quivered in the current. In a minute or so they would reach it.

Suddenly one engine sputtered! And then the other wheezed and coughed and both engines conked out completely!

Terror gripped at Scott's heart. His ears were filled with the roar of the rapids. He saw Antoin and Pierre go into action in grim silence. One pulled with all the strength of his big shoulders at the sweep, the other made the pike-pole quiver as the full weight of his body drove it against the river bottom. Pierre managed to turn the bow from the boulder but, in spite of Antoin's strength, the stern ground against it with a sickening crunch.

The boat gave a lurch. Manty, jerked free from Scott's light hold, shot over the side into the torrent. The boy made a quick grab for him. The next instant he was in the water himself.

Scott came to the surface. Manty was clutched under one arm. But the icy plunge had almost paralyzed the boy. He saw Pierre thrust the pike-pole toward him. He reached for it. But the strong current tugged him toward a whirl-pool. He was sucked under again, still holding on to Manty.

Desperately, he fought against the drag of the under-tow. Kicking his feet and paddling with his free arm, somehow he found strength to move his numbed limbs. He reached the surface. Something solid brushed against his shoulder. Somehow, Antoin had managed to pick up the big sweep and hold it out to him. He threw his arms around it and hung on. Hazily, he felt a strong hand grasp his shirt and heave him and the dripping Manty into the stern of the boat.

Scott lay there, too numbed to move. He could see Antoin swing the steering-sweep into place again. But before there was time to use it a second grinding crash heeled the boat over. A wall of water came surging above the gunnel.

As though in a nightmare, the boy watched Antoin pulling at the steering-sweep. Gradually the boat righted itself. Antoin spoke for the first time since the engines had stopped.

"The gravel bar this side of the willows! It's our only

chance! Quick! The water's coming in fast!"

Scott forced himself groggily to his feet. They were in calm water now and Pierre was heaving grimly at the pike-pole. Antoin had unshipped the sweep and was using it as an ordinary man would use a canoe paddle. But the current was swifter than the smooth surface indicated and the waterlogged craft moved sluggishly.

Scott picked up a spare pole and gritted his teeth as he pushed it against the bottom. He could see that they were moving diagonally across toward the shore, but the current was pulling them downstream at an alarming rate. They were being carried relentlessly toward a huge pile of driftwood, stranded on a bar in midstream. Nobody spoke. Beads of perspiration rolled down Antoin's brows. Even Scott knew that, if the boat was carried against the log-jam, the current would crush it down amongst the tangled snags. There would be little hope of any of them escaping alive.

For what seemed an eternity, their combined efforts resulted only in preventing the boat from being swept backwards by the current. Then it gradually dawned on Scott that they were creeping away from the log-jam at an ever increasing rate. They had reached a back-eddy beyond it! The same current that had all but swept them to their doom now helped to ground the boat on the sheltered bar.

They waded ashore through water up to their waists. Pierre started to whittle shavings from a piece of dry driftwood above high-water mark. Teeth chattering, hands trembling, Scott fished in his pocket for his waterproof match case.

"Manty! Keep back!" the boy yelled as a shower of icy drops extinguished the first match. But Manty shook and shook. Scott had to hold him while Pierre kindled the fire.

Soon the crackling flames were bringing life back to the boy's chilled body. "Come on, Manty," he called soothingly. "Get close to the fire. You can shake all you like now." But the dog kept his distance and bounded into the woods. In a minute or two, they heard the angry scolding of a red squirrel, interspersed with Manty's shrill yelping.

Pierre laughed. "He don't like water. He don't like the fire." Pierre shrugged.

Scott started to laugh, too. "I suppose it's one way to get warm. But darned if I feel like chasing squirrels myself."

Antoin thrashed about in the water, carrying the food supplies and dunnage ashore. When the job was finished, he seemed to be in high spirits. "The kitchen-box and the bags—they were covered with the canvas—nothing got very wet. It will soon dry out." He went on gaily. "The boat is aground and full of water—but your pipe won't melt!"

Scott's spirits sagged, in spite of Antoin's exuberance. "A fat lot of use the pipe will be to my father where it is now," he said wearily. "How long will it take to get help to salvage it?"

"Help!" The riverman echoed. "Antoin doesn't need help, except from Pierre and yourself! Antoin has been in worse trouble than this! By tomorrow night, the boat will be repaired—ready to start out when daylight comes."

Two nights camped on the bar! Scott's mind slowly digested the idea. It could have been worse, he had to admit. Antoin sounded very sure of himself . . . but Scott couldn't imagine how the three of them were going to repair the boat and manhandle the cargo in a day and a half.

All that afternoon and all the next day they worked. They cut long poles to reach the boat's gunnels so they could roll the pipe ashore. They bailed out the boat and swung it broadside onto skids laid on the beach. Prying with levers, alternately at the bow and stern, they zigzagged it onto dry land. Antoin hewed pieces of wood to patch the holes in the hull and sealed the cracks with spruce gum.

By midafternoon the boat was back in the water again and they were ready to reload the pipe. After it was onboard, Scott felt as though his legs would fold up before he got back as far as the campfire. They hadn't been working by the clock. They had worked from dawn to dusk!

Antoin looked down at Scott with admiration in his eyes. "By gosh! You are a fine boy! In the water you swim like a beaver—on land you work like a beaver!"

The riverman sat down and whittled off slices of black plug tobacco and puffed reflectively at his pipe. "Me? I am one big fool. I think nothing ever goes wrong with the engines—always they go along *br-r-r!* So I take the chance on the short cut between the boulders!"

Pierre's dark eyes burned in the firelight as he shot a

puzzled glance at Scott. "How about the kickers stopping like that? It doesn't figure."

"The ignition . . ." Scott hazarded.

Pierre interrupted, shaking his head. "Each engine has a separate ignition."

"Dirty spark plugs?"

"All four plugs wouldn't go haywire at once!" Pierre gazed into the fire for a few moments.

Suddenly he put down his empty coffee cup and jumped to his feet. "I'll tell you what, Scott. The flashlight in the grub-box is still working. You come and hold it while I have a look at the engines."

The boys climbed onboard the boat. Pierre uncoupled a length of copper tubing from the gas tank and put it to his mouth. When he blew through it, a shower of bead-like drops spattered on the floor boards.

"Water!" He took a pail and held it under the valve leading from the main gas tank. When he turned the valve, a clear liquid flowed into the pail. It was almost full before the beam of the flashlight lit up a thin, oily slick clouding the surface.

Scott gulped and the rays of the flashlight wavered as his hand started to shake. The liquid in the pail must be water . . . but how? Why?

"Hey, Papa!" Pierre's words burst out in a childish treble, unbelief turning to bewilderment. "Come and look at this. Nearly four gallons of water in the tank!"

The boat shook from stem to stern as Antoin scrambled onboard. His rage was terrifying to behold. "This is the work of crooks! I will make a trip to the coast and find the rascal who sold us this water! I will pour it down his throat! I will push his head in a bucket. Water! I will give him water. A few drops of water in the gas sometimes —that can't be helped. But a bucket of water in one drum of gas—that is robbery!"

Antoin extended an outstretched hand as though he were about to grasp somebody by the throat. Then he hunched his massive shoulders and turned his back on the boys. The makeshift gangway of poles creaked under his weight as he went ashore.

Pierre turned to Scott and said, "We can push the flashlight under the lashings . . . like this. Now you won't have to hold it. I'll clear the gas lines. Let's see, here's a wrench that will fit the plugs. You can take them out and clean the points."

For the next half hour, as the boys worked at the engines, the long northern twilight gradually closed in around them. Scott could hear Antoin grumbling to himself as he filled his pipe. "A gang of crooks! That's what they are!"

Who are the mysterious "they"? Scott asked himself. Of course, Antoin means the company who supplied his gas. But could there be a gang involved? If so, could they be the same people who planned the wreck of the cat-train? The boy shrugged the thought off. He was too tired to think about it.

When Scott and Pierre finally went ashore, the fire had died down to glowing embers. Antoin's anger seemed to have faded as the flickering flames went out.

Pierre yawned, "I guess we can call it a day."

"You can say that again! Good night, fellows." Scott crawled into his sleeping bag. He wasn't awake long enough to go over all the events of the last two days in his mind. We came through the rapids the hard way . . . it will be all plain sailing tomorrow . . . Osprey Creek before noon . . .

There was no sound in his ears but the lapping of the river on the gravel as Scott fell asleep.

13

FLASH FLOOD AT OSPREY CREEK

THE purr of the engines was like music in Scott's ears the next morning as they raced the current downstream. He had helped Pierre tune the kickers up, so that now they seemed to sing a song of triumph while the boat glided along the smooth, swift water below the rapids.

Scott leaned back against the dunnage in the bow and listened to the steady drone that never faltered. Trees along the bank marched backwards, like a guard of honor saluting him as he neared his destination. At last the kickers stopped with a satisfied snort. The boat with its precious cargo of pipe was alongside the landing at the mouth of Osprey Creek!

The singing still seemed to be in his ears; the noonday sun blazed down from an azure sky. His father reached down from the wharf and clasped his hand.

"Well, Son! What on earth happened to you?"

"Gosh! Dad, it's a long story. But I brought the pipe."

His father's hand squeezed his shoulder. "Good work! You got my letter, all right?"

"Tim Donovan gave it to me as soon as the *Chutine* got in. He said you needed gas for the sawmill, but I talked him into shipping the pipe first."

"That's the stuff! The pipe was what we needed. We'll be able to work double shifts now."

Manty, after a hurried examination of the dock, dashed in between them. He snorted nervously at Mr. Haliburton and looked around questioningly at Scott.

Mr. Haliburton snapped his fingers. "Hullo, there— what's your name?"

"This is Manty," Scott hastened to explain. "He was nearly killed by the big dogs on the trail. I looked after him and he decided I belonged to him. Wow! I have a lot of things to tell you. . . ."

Mr. Haliburton knelt down. Manty sniffed at his hand and allowed him to pat his head. "Smart little chap—isn't he? I'm glad he picked you."

Dave Haliburton got up and moved toward the dock. A half a dozen miners were setting planks in place to unload the cargo. The boy could hear Antoin in the boat, bellowing to them. "Gas like that . . . robbery! It could have been . . . murder!" The big riverman was punctuating his remarks by pounding his fist on the gas tank.

"Hi, Antoin! Pierre!" Mr. Haliburton cut in. "When you get the unloading started, come up to the office." With a friendly wave of his hand, he started away from the dock before Antoin had time to reply.

"Now let's go up to the mine and you can tell me about your trip." Mr. Haliburton beckoned his son to follow him. He led the way along a trail through the jackpine and aspens bordering the creek. After ten minutes they emerged onto a narrow flat. The boy saw four buildings of fresh-cut lumber, which looked out of place against a backdrop of green hills.

"There you are, Son—office, bunkhouse, mess hall and blacksmith shop."

But Scott was looking beyond the buildings at a great, bare scar on the hillside.

"That's where we're sluicing," his father explained. "You can see the pipeline coming down from the dam in the distance. You can't see the monitors from here because of those big heaps of gravel and boulders near the edge of the creek. That's the tailing dump—it's been slowing us down a lot. But now we have the extra pipe, we'll be able to rig a third monitor to sluice it out of the way."

Mr. Haliburton pushed open the door of the office. "Now! Make yourself comfortable and let's have the whole story."

"Remember the Jack o' Diamonds claim on Magpie Creek." The words unfolded from Scott's memory without faltering.

A quick frown crinkled Mr. Haliburton's brow. He jumped to his feet and slammed the door shut.

"Where did you? How?" Mr. Haliburton's words trailed off.

"Captain Dan told me to give you that message," Scott said.

His father flung himself down on a chair and sat staring at the brass gold scales on the desk. Scott's eyes were drawn in the same direction. How many ounces of the precious metal would be weighed up on those scales before the season was over? Enough to make the venture worth while? He wondered.

"What was the Jack o' Diamonds?" Scott asked.

"It turned out to be one of the richest claims in the north, but the man who staked it had a run of bad luck and sold it for a song. He found out too late that he had been the victim of a gang of crooks. He was never able to prove anything against them."

"Gosh! And Captain Dan thinks something like that might happen here?"

"He wants us to be on the lookout for trouble, at any rate." Dave Haliburton looked at his son with a smile that was faintly apologetic. "To tell the truth, if anyone had turned up to try and buy the mine before you arrived with that pipe, I would have been tempted to let it go for almost nothing."

Scott mused, "I wonder why the captain didn't write you a note."

"Captain Dan sees everybody who goes up the river," Mr. Haliburton said slowly. "He must have a strong suspicion about some of them. He might have been afraid that my mail would be tampered with."

"Tampered with!" Scott repeated. "One of the things I have to tell you is that my rock collection was stolen from my dunnage bag." His voice rose with excitement.

His father sat bolt upright. "It was! When?"

"Not in the Cassiar." Scott spoke more calmly. "I've thought it over and they must have been taken before my bag came on board at Wrangell."

Mr. Haliburton looked puzzled and shook his head. "Why should anyone want those bits of rock? Anyway, it couldn't have any connection with the captain's message, if they were taken before you boarded the *Chutine.*"

Scott shrugged. "I figured it was the work of a sneak thief."

His father nodded in agreement. "Now," he said, "tell me why you took so long to get here. What was Antoin ranting about when we left the dock? Did he run out of gas?"

Scott plunged into the story of the last two days.

"Queer!" his father commented. "How on earth could that much water get into the gas tank? Why didn't Pierre notice it when they gassed up? He's not blind."

Scott remained silent, gnawing at his lower lip. Since he had left the coast, there seemed to be no end to the questions that still went unanswered.

His father shot a keen questioning glance at him. "That only accounts for two days. The boat was at least a week later than I'd expected."

Scott hesitated. How much should he tell? Constable Black had warned him not to talk.

Before Scott could speak, Antoin came storming in. Pierre winked at Scott as the riverman launched into a repetition of his plans to exact retribution from the people who supplied his gasoline. Mr. Haliburton obviously found it hard to conceal his impatience as Antoin delivered a colorful account of the swamping in the rapids. But he became suddenly alert when the riverman roared, "And that is not all—the cat-train rolled a thousand feet into Tuya Canyon!"

Scott found it a relief to have the boatman pour out his own dramatic version of the accident. Constable Black had said not to mention a word to anybody about the brake-rope. If he had told the story himself, Scott could imagine his father asking, "Did Tim have any ideas *why* the rope broke?" But now, Antoin's vivid imagination appeared to have left nothing unsaid. The rope obviously had been chafed by rubbing against the top-load—so said Antoin, who hadn't been there.

Scott glanced up eagerly when he heard the clang of metal against an iron bar coming from the direction of the mess hall. "Come and get it!" the cook shouted. Scott was ravenously hungry. As far as he was concerned, there was no need for the cook to add, ". . . or I'll throw it away!"

Even Antoin stopped talking when Mr. Haliburton invited him to have lunch with them. Scott entered the dining room behind his father, hesitating for a minute or two in confusion as his father introduced each of the ten men at the long table by name. The boy forgot each name almost immediately. No matter, he decided, he would soon get to know the names of these men and the ones in the other shift. At the moment, he was more interested in eating.

Scott soon learned one name: Lars—the big, mild-mannered man sitting next to him. Mr. Haliburton explained, "Lars is the foreman. He'll soon find a job for you."

Scott tucked away generous helpings of roast moose meat and scarcely noticed that there were no fresh vegetables or fruit on the table. There was little conversation during the meal. The miners went back to the bunkhouse as soon as they were finished and Antoin, followed by Pierre, headed for the landing.

The boy waited on the steps for Lars to come out. What would his first job be? He hoped it might be working around the sluices where, perhaps, he would catch glimpses of golden nuggets shining in the wet gravel. But his dreams were shattered when Lars appeared and led him around to the kitchen door. Scott looked at the pile of stove wood lengths of jackpine without enthusiasm.

Lars asked, "Can you handle an ax?"

"Sure!"

"Well, there's enough wood here to keep you going for a while. When you have it all split, we'll get the gas buzz saw working and saw up some more logs. A lot depends on this wood pile. We can't mine gold unless we keep the crew happy. And we won't have a happy crew unless they're well fed. And the cook can't turn out good meals if he runs short of wood."

The job didn't sound so dull when Lars put things that way. Scott's face relaxed in a grin. He picked up the ax and went to work. When he ate his supper that night, he felt he had earned it.

Later, in the office, his father explained to him how they would extend the pipeline from the dam down to the tailing dump. The new pipe would be put together by driving the end of each length a short distance into the next length, in the same way that stove piping was put together. Mr. Haliburton had scarcely finished explaining when Antoin appeared to pick up the mail. They talked for a few minutes about the handful of trappers and prospectors who lived farther down-river, and about the trading post near the forks where the Dease joined the Liard River.

Finally, Antoin jumped to his feet. "I must go. We must bring food down the river for the boy who works like a beaver. *Au revoir!* Before you are awake in the morning, we will be away—*br-r-r-r!*"

"So long for now." Scott stifled a yawn. "I'll take my dunnage over to the bunkhouse and turn in now, Dad."

"Good night, Son."

Scott crept quietly into the bunkhouse. There appeared to be somebody sound asleep in every bunk but his own. Scott was so tired that he crawled into his sleeping bag and not even the varied chorus of snoring could keep him awake.

The boy was kept busy during the days that followed. At first he developed painful blisters on his palms, but after two weeks his hands hardened and he mastered the heft of the ax. After three weeks he was beginning to stack up neat piles of stove wood and was drawing well ahead of the cook's requirements.

Every ten days or so there would be a little flurry of excitement when Antoin returned with supplies and mail. The second mail brought news that Bunny would soon be on his feet again. In the meantime, another cat-skinner had been hired to haul the new wagons that had arrived on the *Chutine*.

To this Antoin added, "But soon they won't need the cat—they won't need the horses. The government, she's going to make a road out of the trail. With cats—three days! But with trucks—perhaps three hours!"

Sometimes the boat stopped just long enough to deliver mail and then continued with freight for the trading posts downstream. It would be three or four days before it returned and always Antoin had the same story. "Next trip—then McTavish, he's coming out for his holiday."

Every time Antoin said that, Scott hoped very hard it was true. McTavish was the trader Jack expected to relieve. If the trader came out, Scott would see Jack on his way in.

But Antoin's visits served only to underline the steady routine of work that went on at the mine. Scott was often called on to help Lars in the blacksmith shop now, or to carry tools up to the monitors. That was always a thrill —to watch the miners swing the big nozzles back and forth as the powerful jets bored into the hillside. The clay and gravel seemed to melt like brown sugar and slide into the sluice, which was a wide, open-topped box of rough planks. Across the bottom of the last section of the sluices, there were bars of angle-iron, called riffles, between which the gold settled. But the lighter gravel and sand were swept on over the riffles to the tailing dump.

Watching the monitors at work seemed to hold a fascination, even to Lars. "That's an old channel where the creek used to run between those two hills that we're cutting into now. There'll be gold there, all right, but perhaps we won't be able to get at it. We need water power to keep going. By Jimminy! The way the creek's going down, I don't know how we can keep going. Did you notice how the water dropped today?"

"Yes." Scott was puzzled. "A foot at least . . . but why?"

Lars's china-blue eyes stared unblinkingly up at the mountains. "Who knows? There's been rain—I heard a clap of thunder in the hills yesterday. The water should be rising. Perhaps there's been a slide upstream. If there has, it's not likely there's much we can do about it."

A slide upstream? Scott wondered. Could this be a sample of the so-called "run of bad luck" that had plagued the Jack o' Diamonds claim? He knew that when his father and Lars cleaned out the riffles every second day, the clean-up had weighed heavier each time. Now, as they walked back along the creek, Scott could see boulders in midstream, bared by the falling water. For some unaccountable reason, the mine's lifeblood seemed to be drying up.

Lars said, "We'll have to shut down one of the monitors tomorrow. This placer mining is always a gamble. You know, Scott, somewhere up in the mountains, there must be the quartz where this gold we're mining came from."

"The Mother Lode?"

"Ay! Perhaps." Lars shrugged. "Scott, you're a lot younger than I am. Some day you'll have a chance to get up in the mountains. Around the six thousand foot level, you'll see the serpentine rock. Mark my words! That's where nature has stored her treasures. Perhaps it's the Mother Lode—perhaps it's something more valuable than gold."

Scott was impressed by Lars's knowledge. He seemed to know all about rock. He had never been to a university, but from practical experience, he knew the significance of buried channels . . . and . . . and . . . serpentine? Doubts fluttered in the boy's mind. Lars's remarks about the serpentine had an unrealistic, dreamlike quality— as though he weren't quite sure of himself.

A few minutes later, Scott was in the office, studying the maps on the wall. There, sure enough, was the word *serpentine,* printed in red letters across the mountains at the head of Osprey Creek. What was its significance? Would he ever understand what lay behind that and all the other rock formations marked on the map? Was the mine going to pay well enough so that his father could help him to take the university training he needed? Or when he was older, would he still have gaps in his knowledge, as Lars had?

Suddenly the foreman was at the door. "Dave, the creek is so low now there's no run-off to fill the dam!"

"Probably a landslide upstream." Mr. Haliburton's brow crinkled with a puzzled frown. "Let's hope it will back the water up and clear itself in a day or two. Meanwhile, we can take advantage of the low water. Put the men to work, plugging those leaks in the dam."

Next morning, Osprey Creek had shrunk to a mere trickle that a man could wade across in hip boots. Dave Haliburton's face was lined with sorry. "It would take more than an ordinary slide to do this, Son. There must have been a rock slide in the upper canyon. It could shut us down for the rest of the season, if we don't get heavy rains."

Scott swallowed hard. If that happened, he supposed his father would have to sell the mine . . . University would be out of the question then. It all sounded so much like the story of the Jack o' Diamonds! Trying to sound cheerful, Scott said, "Lars heard a clap of thunder in the hills yesterday."

The ghost of a smile appeared on his father's face. "Well, a clap of thunder should be a good sign—even if there isn't a cloud in the sky."

But, by lunch time, black clouds were rolling down into the valley. They blotted out the distant mountains and dimmed the near-by hills in gray haze. Two hours later, the heavens seemed to open up. A steady downpour continued until evening, but the trickle in the creek-bed rose only an inch or two.

There was a tense air of expectancy amongst the men in the bunkhouse as darkness began to close in on the camp. No one made any attempt to turn in. Small groups of oilskin clad miners kept wandering down to the banks of the creek to watch the inch by inch rise of the water.

Scott had crossed the flats to the creek with three other men when suddenly a muffled roaring rumbled down the valley. Looking up, he saw, scarcely visible in the twilight, a foam-flecked crest of brown water surge around the tailing dump. "Great Snakes! Here it comes!" one of the men shouted. "Let's get out of here!"

Muddy water was already surging around his rubber boots as Scott followed the three miners in a wild scramble toward the buildings. Out of the corner of his eyes, he saw uprooted trees and planks from the sluices careening down the swelling creek.

Knee-deep water suddenly welled into a hollow in front of him. He plunged through it and a few moments later, he reached the bunkhouse. The weather-beaten faces of the miners showed strangely white in the gloom. A score of eyes were fixed on the mounting torrent.

Then everyone was galvanized into action by Mr. Haliburton shouting, "Shake it up! Get your dunnage out of the bunkhouse and take it up to the pine-flats!"

Scott rushed to his bunk and threw his loose gear into his bag. Then, with it under his arm and his sleeping bag over his shoulder, he struggled up the slope. Slipping and sliding, he came back down the hill.

"Move the supplies out of the mess hall—you two look for tarps to cover them!" Mr. Haliburton took the lead in executing the brisk orders he issued.

After two more trips, Scott's feet began to feel like leaden weights. The cases of canned goods seemed to pull his shoulders loose from their sockets each time he staggered uphill to the pine-ridge. Amongst the pines, the white glare of a gas lantern shimmered on the wet oilskins of the miners as they stacked up the precious food supplies.

Back in the mess house, another lantern cast its beams out across water that looked black and oily where it lapped only a few inches below the doorsill. This slow spreading of the turbid water toward the buildings seemed more terrifying to Scott than the thundering crest that had first swept over the lower sluices.

He heard a series of splashes as a tier of the woodpile collapsed. His woodpile! Three weeks of his work drifting off into the darkness, and he was powerless to save it!

And the water had only to rise another foot to destroy the buildings! That would mean the loss of three years' work—of planning and scrimping and saving. The loss of everything for Scott's father!

The boy started uphill with another box, feeling dazed and discouraged. There was neither excitement nor satisfaction in this retreat from the mill-pond smooth water.

Scott had to force himself to smile when his father called out, "Chin up, Son! Looks as if it's going to come over the floors, but we'll be all right, camped up on the flats."

Scott delivered his load, but he still felt weighted down as he made his way back to the buildings. Then, suddenly, there was a shout from Lars. It made Scott straighten up and discover that he could still smile.

"Dave! The water's starting to drop! The buildings are as safe as . . . as . . ."

"As safe as houses!" Scott suggested with a grin.

14

JACK ARRIVES AT THE MINE

Morning dawned with a few puffs of white cloud floating in a turquoise sky. The early sunlight glinted on dark blue water streaking down Osprey Creek. Except for a few pieces of driftwood on the wet gravel near the buildings and the vacant space where the woodpile once stood, Scott would never have known that anything had happened.

The boy watched the miners climbing up toward the dam with axes and shovels on their shoulders. He knew that the high water had washed away some of the clay-and-log cribbing and that they were going up to repair the damage. With a twinge of envy that he couldn't go with them, he turned to his own job.

He had hard work ahead of him now. The flood had not only damaged the dam and carried away the lower sections of the sluice, but it had overturned the buzz saw. The cylinder casting had hit a rock and developed a crack which Lars said couldn't be repaired.

"You'll have to use this five-foot 'Chinook' crosscut

saw," the foreman told Scott. "It's got weight to it—I'll keep it sharp and you'll find it'll almost do the work by itself."

Scott rolled a log onto the sawhorse and started to saw it into stove wood lengths. He was on the third cut when Lars came back.

"Golly, Lars!" he panted. "This isn't as easy as you made it sound."

"Gently does it," Lars advised him. "Don't fight the saw—let it work at its own speed."

"I'll try," Scott promised. But it took him three difficult days before he realized what Lars meant. At last he got the knack of swinging back and forth, keeping the blade straight in the cut, while the long teeth of the saw bit into the soft pine. By the time the dinner gong sounded that first day, he estimated he had at least two days' supply of wood in the new pile he was starting.

Soon after the evening meal was over, Scott heard the hum of the boat's engines coming from downriver. He hurried to the landing and waited impatiently while the boat crawled in against the current. There was no sign of a passenger! What news would Antoin have of the trader this time?

Scott found out as soon as the boat touched the dock. Antoin shouted, "McTavish! He's bushed for sure. Now he says he will wait for next year for his holiday."

The boy pretended to echo Antoin's laughter, but he turned and walked back to the office with a heavy heart. He wouldn't be seeing Jack, after all. But some of the things he had counted on might still come true.

"Dad," Scott asked anxiously, "suppose I work like the dickens and get all the wood cut—how about you and I taking a trip up into the mountains?"

"I'd like to, Son." His father looked worried and tired. "But everything depends on these next few weeks. I don't feel I should leave the mine, even for a few days. However, we'll see later."

Scott frowned—his father didn't sound very hopeful.

In the meantime, the miners had repaired the dam. Jets of water were gushing again from the monitors. Scott thought that certainly, now that they were assured of full water power, they should soon find out if there was gold in the old channel.

A few days later, as the boy sat in the office, eagerly watching his father weigh the clean-up, Mr. Haliburton looked up with a smile. "We're into real pay-dirt at last!" he declared. He poured a glittering stream of gold dust from the pan of the scales to a buckskin sack. It looked almost like coarse sawdust, but it was heavier than lead. "Some of the nuggets in this lot will be worth between twenty-five and fifty dollars apiece."

Before Scott had time to answer, Manty sprang to his feet. He froze stiff-legged, his hackles bristling, and growled a warning deep down in his throat. Looking out through the door, Scott recognized two figures silhouetted in the twilight.

"It's Gold Brick and Tommy Naas."

Mr. Haliburton turned toward the door. Scott noticed that Gold Brick's clothes were rumpled and soiled, but his face had the same old cocky expression as he strode up the path.

"Hi, Scotty!" Gold Brick didn't wait for an invitation to come in. "Pleased to meet you, Dave—I've heard a lot about you." He thrust out his hand. "That accident at the Tuya was a tough break, wasn't it?"

"That wasn't the only one," Mr. Haliburton said evenly. "I guess you haven't heard about Antoin's engine conking out in the rapids. He came close to losing the boat and cargo."

Scott kept his eyes fixed on Gold Brick but he could detect no change in his expression.

His father went on. "And then last week we had a flash flood that held us up for a few days."

Gold Brick was seldom at a loss for words. But now he spoke very slowly. Scott got the impression that he was choosing his words very carefully.

"We came through Blueberry Pass," he said, "and down Handy Creek. When we hit Osprey I noticed it had been up over the high-water mark. I suppose it was a landslide —that's liable to happen on a big creek like this that heads so far back in the mountains."

"I suppose." Mr. Haliburton settled back in his chair and waited to hear what else Gold Brick had to say. There was a second or two of silence. Then Gold Brick was talking again, in his usual glib, self-assured fashion. The words came out so smoothly that Scott found himself wondering if they had been rehearsed.

"Like drawing to an inside straight, isn't it? You can't depend on supplies getting in and you can't depend on the water supply. It's too big a risk for one man to take. If it was split up amongst a group of men who could afford to lose a little money, it wouldn't be so bad."

"Not bad at all for them. They could pick up a little easy money, now that I've already taken all the risks." Mr. Haliburton appeared to be mildly amused.

Gold Brick persisted as though he hadn't been interrupted. "You know better than that. In gold mining there's no end to the risks you have to take. Now, I've a proposition: I have some good contacts down south. Set your price and give me your power of attorney. I'll go out on the next boat and make a deal for you."

"You're wasting your time, Schnider. I have no idea of selling out!" When his father's jaw set like that, Scott knew he meant it.

Gold Brick rose to his feet. "Okay—it's up to you. The Indian and I are going back up to Handy Creek to do some work on a prospect up there. If you change your mind, you'll know where to find me."

Mr. Haliburton's tone was cordial enough as he offered the normal hospitality of the North. "Drop into the mess hall and the cook will serve you some prime moose steaks. We're lucky when it comes to meat. We have a permit from the Game Board to kill one moose a week. And we have an old Casca Indian, Hunter Sam, who never lets us down."

After the two men disappeared, Mr. Haliburton turned to his son. "Now that message of Captain Dan's about the Jack o' Diamonds claim begins to make sense."

"Gee, Dad! Do you mean that Gold Brick is a crook?"

Mr. Haliburton shook his head. "Nothing crooked about wanting to buy a mine. Let's just say that Schnider is a smart operator."

A host of memories of his trip were buzzing in Scott's head. "Gee-whizz—do you suppose it could have been Gold Brick who stole my rock samples?"

"They wouldn't have been much use to him, would they?"

"No . . . I suppose not." Scott said no more. But he couldn't shake from his mind the picture of Gold Brick on the dock at Telegraph Creek, saying that he was having Scott's dunnage sent up to the hotel. He recalled Constable Black, dropping in at Tim's to ask about the "character with the nugget jewelry."

As the summer days slipped by, the puzzle about Gold Brick remained unsolved. About every two weeks, Schnider would come down the creek to see if Antoin had left any mail for him. But he never stayed long and he had surprisingly little to say.

By the end of July, Scott's pile of split wood had grown bigger than the stack of uncut logs. His muscles seemed to have grown with the woodpile. There wasn't an ounce of surplus fat on the boy's body, yet all his clothes seemed to be a little too small for him.

From now on, he worked only two or three hours a day at the wood. The rest of the time Scott usually spent in the shop with Lars. He learned to handle a sledge hammer, to grind a point on a pick and to file a razor edge on an axe. He tried to master the art of sharpening the crosscut saw, but the foreman was critical of his efforts.

"You've got the idea," Lars said, "but you need practice to teach you to hold the file level."

Scott worked away at the saw with a frown of concentration on his brow, tip of his tongue showing at the corner of his mouth. His first three attempts still had to be touched up by Lars. But at last he managed to file each tooth to a sharp point at the proper bevel and to even up the height of each raker between the teeth.

But he did not lose interest in his new collection of rock samples. Often, after work was over, he climbed to the upper benches with a geologist's pick in his hand and Manty at his heels. The dog barked furiously at chattering squirrels, or searched out grouse that exploded from the thickets in a flurry of whirring wings, while Scott chipped off fragments from interesting looking rock outcroppings with his pick. He added to his collection, but he knew there was no chance of finding the Mother Lode in these near-by hills.

Every time Scott spoke of going into the mountains, his father said, "We'll see how things turn out. At present we're too busy mining to go chasing rainbows." And here it was the middle of August; the summer wild flowers had been replaced by orange tiger lilies and red spikes of Indian paintbrush. And the frost had already touched the leaves of the aspens and mountain maples, delicately and gently, but enough to overlay the green with a tinge of yellow.

Tonight or tomorrow, the boat should arrive. The freight was nearly all delivered to the interior now and it would be almost two weeks before Antoin returned. And when he did, Scott would have to go back with him. It would be his last chance to be out in time for school.

Scott was in the office when they heard the drone of the boat pulling into the landing. Mr. Haliburton had just spread the clean-up for the last three days out in a copper scoop. His son was separating the black sand from the gold dust with a magnet. This black sand was the only substance heavy enough to stay in the riffles with the gold but, being a compound of iron, it was attracted to a magnet and it was not too difficult to remove.

It was a good clean-up, just about the weight they had expected. But Mr. Haliburton looked puzzled. "It's odd, Son, that we get so few nuggets. Yesterday I was almost sure I saw three big ones, glittering under the water at the bottom of the sluices."

Scott stared at his father. "Gee, Dad!" he exclaimed. "Do you think someone is high-grading them? Should we clean-up every day, instead of every three days?"

"What do you think?" His father countered. "You know the crew as well, or better, than I do. Is there anyone you think would rob the sluices?"

Scott considered the question seriously. "No, Dad," he answered slowly. "Come to think of it, there's no one —absolutely no one."

His father rose and put his hand on his son's shoulder. "Don't feel badly, Son. Besides, I may be mistaken. Running water plays strange tricks on your eyes. I may have been letting my imagination run away with me. Come on —we'll go down and see Antoin."

As they neared the landing, Scott noticed that Antoin had brought a passenger this trip. That was odd—they weren't expecting anybody at the mine. The stranger had his back to them, but there was something familiar about his stocky figure. Scott ran for a few paces and then slowed to a walk. It couldn't possibly be—McTavish hadn't come out, there was no chance of Jack arriving.

Then Antoin's passenger climbed onto the dock. Scott sprinted as fast as his legs would carry him. It was Jack! The boy did a little jig as he reached the dock. "Boy, oh boy! Am I glad to see you! How under the sun did you manage to get here?"

Before Jack had time to answer, a big tawny dog with a scrawny tail leaped out of the boat with an angry snarl. Jack struggled to retain his hold on the animal's collar. Manty dashed forward and pranced back and forth, barely keeping out of reach of snapping teeth.

"Hi there!" Jack gasped. "Watch that little pooch, or he'll get eaten up!"

Scott scooped Manty up in his arms. "Cut it out!" he ordered. Manty's shrill barking subsided. Scott said, "That's better. Now say hullo to Jack and . . . and . . . why it's Dinty!"

The boy felt a sudden lump in his throat. There was only one possible explanation of why Beaver's one-man dog could be here with Jack. He looked questioningly at Dinty's new master.

Jack nodded solemnly. "Beaver started downriver alone. His kicker must have been swamped in a big swell at Buck's Bar. His boat washed ashore, but Dinty wouldn't let anyone near it until I got there with the constable."

Scott let Manty go. Dinty wagged his tail and started to play with the little dog as a cat plays with a kitten.

"Beaver told me at Steamboat Bend the river would get him some day," said Scott.

"We buried him on a jackpine bench, overlooking the river," Jack said quietly. "The wind roaring through the pines sounded like organ music, and the river rolling by seemed as though it would go on for ever and ever. I . . . well . . . it sort of makes you think about things."

Scott murmured, "I guess he wouldn't have wanted it any other way. He was about the last of the old-timers. There aren't many like him left."

"No, the country's changing fast—even in the weeks since you came in, Scott. That trail's almost a road now! You'd hardly believe it. The government sent bulldozers and graders and they're working on it like nobody's business." Jack glanced around as though to make sure that no one else was within earshot. He went on quietly. "For the record—if anyone wants to know what I'm doing here, I have an outfit of trade goods. There's supposed to be a nomadic band of Bear Lake Indians coming down Osprey Creek. Officially, that's why I'm here. The rest I'll tell you later."

Just then, Mr. Haliburton, having finished talking to Antoin, came over and joined them. Scott introduced Jack to his father and the three of them started up toward the mine. Scott shot sidelong glances at his friend, trying to fathom what all the air of mystery was about. Hunter Sam had told him about the Bear Lakers, who often came down Osprey Creek. These wandering Indians seemed a logical reason for the arrival of a fur trader.

The next hour seemed endless to Scott as he sat in the office, listening to Jack making arrangements with Mr. Haliburton for permission to erect a big tent near the mine buildings in which to store his trade goods. At last, when everything was settled, Scott was able to make the excuse that he'd take Jack up to see the monitors.

The boy barely contained his curiosity until they were out of earshot of the miners in the bunkhouse. "Let's have it," he demanded. "What's 'the rest' that you were going to tell me later?"

"It's about the brake-rope. . . ."

"Huh?" Scott gulped. What did Jack know about the rope, he wondered.

As if he had read Scott's thoughts, Jack said, "Okay —I know you weren't supposed to talk about it. But I'm in on the deal now. The constable sent those two ends out to the police laboratory and found out they had some kind of goo on them. Grease it was—the kind of grease they use on Norse sheath knives to keep them from rusting."

"But . . . how did you get into the act?"

A faint smile flickered across Jack's face. "I'm number one witness. We received a shipment of those knives the day I arrived. I sold three of them on the boat day—one to Gold Brick, one to Tommy Naas and one to Gee-gee. Tommy and Gold Brick were out in the hills by the time the report came back. But I remembered Gold Brick must have left his in a box of supplies in the store overnight, because when he came in the next morning, he held the knife up and said, 'They sure use a good grade of steel in these things.' "

"Golly!" That seemed to put Gold Brick in the clear. Scott's mind was in a whirl. "Did the constable question Gee-gee?" he asked.

"Yes. All the old man had to say was that he didn't remember when he first used the knife—said he plumb forgot."

Scott's voice trembled with frustration. "Why in heck couldn't Gee-gee give a better answer than that? I figure it must have been Tommy who cut the rope. His tribe are old enemies of the Tahltans. He could have been out to get Jimmy Brokenose—his grandfather was a Tahltan chief. I'm almost sure Tommy was the fellow who rushed past so quietly when we were clearing the water supply at Telegraph Creek. He has a mug shaped just like the one I glimpsed in the tank. He might have been sneaking down to the wagons then."

Jack shrugged. "Maybe so—but it's not much to go on."

"Gee-gee did make a crack about being in wrong with the police," Scott murmured. "But I don't think it can be anything very serious. Gee-gee is a good hombre as far as I'm concerned."

"Me, too!" Jack agreed warmly. "I think Tommy probably had something to do with the accident. Perhaps Gold Brick, too, in spite of his alibi. My boss talked things over with the constable. He's anxious to find out the answer, because his post sold the knives. So, that's why I'm here—to look dumb and keep my eyes open for a couple of weeks."

15

INTO THE MOUNTAINS

Whe two boys got back to the office, they found Mr. Haliburton reading his mail. He looked up with a smile as they entered the room.

"This should interest you, Son," he said, indicating the letter he had before him. "Would you like to go out by plane?"

"Wow! Would I ever?"

"Well, here's your chance. Dr. Lawson, the government geologist for this district, is flying in to make a report on the mine. His plane will land on Summit Lake. That's about fifteen miles up Osprey Creek. Can't come here where the river's too narrow and winding for a safe landing. He says he can carry an extra passenger on the southbound flight, if we've anyone who wants to go."

"Oh, boy!" Scott exclaimed. "Here's somebody who wants to go."

Mr. Haliburton went on, "You'll get out to the railway line in a few hours. That means you'll be able to stay four or five days after the boat leaves and still be

163

home in time for school opening."

"An extra four or five days! Golly! Now we'll be able to make that trip into the mountains, won't we? Please, Dad!" Scott felt excitement rising within him so quickly that he could hardly get the words out.

But his father shook his head slowly. "I'm sorry, Son. With Dr. Lawson due to make his report, I don't want to leave the mine now. You could go up the creek with Hunter Sam for a few days' fishing if you like. But I wouldn't want you to go into the mountains—with one old Indian and a cayuse that has seen better days, there's no telling what sort of trouble you might get into. Suppose you fell and broke a leg or something."

"Aw, heck!" Scott was not rebellious, but bitterly disappointed.

Mr. Haliburton continued. "Of course, if Jack weren't tied down to that store-in-a-tent he's opening up—if he could go with you—that would be different."

Jack spoke up in a crisp, businesslike tone. "My instructions are not to let the grass grow under my feet. I'd be glad of a chance to get out and see if there is any sign of the Indians being on the move. I'd be combining business with pleasure if I went into the mountains with Scott."

Scott looked eagerly at his father. "We could start in about a week. I'll have all the wood cut by that time."

"In a week then. We'll arrange things to fit in with Hunter Sam's next hunt." Dave Haliburton's voice was just as businesslike as Jack's. "Well, we'll talk over the details of your outfit later. Good night, boys."

Everything had been settled so quickly that Scott was in

a daze as he and Jack left the office. On the way to the bunkhouse, the boy felt as though he were already flying. For a moment, before he yielded to the pleasant sensation, he had one little twinge of regret: he had been looking forward to the trip downriver on the *Chutine* with Captain Dan. However, he decided you couldn't have it both ways —and the opportunity of looking down on the Cassiar Mountains from the air was something literally "out of this world."

In Scott's dreams that night he was up near the clouds, but not in a plane. He was plodding up a mountainside, and he was using his geologist's pick to break off chips of rock that were streaked with gold.

All next morning Scott zipped the heavy, five-foot saw back and forth. A buzz saw, he said to himself, has nothing on me.

Just before lunch he was startled by a deep voice behind him. "Easy, young fellow! That saw's just about smokin'."

"Gee-gee!"

Scott wheeled around to see the familiar bow-legged walk and the long-barreled revolver swinging in its holster.

"Gee-gee! I'm sure glad to see you." He laid the saw down across the few remaining logs. "Come into the mess-house. You're just in time for lunch."

"Thank you—you won't have to ask me twice," boomed Gee-gee. "Been on the trail for three weeks. Packin' in supplies to some prospectors in the Big Muddy country. Decided to come back this way."

"Come on then." Scott led the way to the mess-house.

"You've grown some since I saw you last," Gee-gee rumbled. "There's muscles in your arms I never noticed before." His glance swept over the boy approvingly.

Scott grinned as he poured water into the tin basin to wash up. "And you look younger than ever, Old-timer," he said warmly.

I'm not kidding, Scott said to himself as he sloshed water on his face. Gee-gee is all right—you only have to look him in the eye to see that he isn't the sort of man who would do a sneaky trick like cutting that brake-rope.

"Well—well! The very man I've been wanting to see!" Scott wiped the soap off his eyes to see his father coming through the door. Mr. Haliburton sat down at the table. "What shape are your cayuses in?" he asked Gee-gee. Without waiting for a reply, he went on, "Do you think you could pack some timbers and some pipe fittings up to the dam? The grade's too steep for that little tractor we use for hauling supplies up from the river."

"Why sure!" Gee-gee sounded mightily pleased with himself. "My pack-string can climb hills that a mountain goat would shy at. How much is there . . ." The old man stopped suddenly as Jack rushed into the dining room.

Scott could see undisguised surprise on Gee-gee's face. "Hullo, Gee-gee," said Jack. "Did Scott tell you I'm all set to trade with that band of Bear Lakers who are coming this way?"

Gee-gee's eyes narrowed as he peered questioningly at Jack. "Sounds like a lot of foolishness to me," he growled. "They'll have sold all their fur at the posts farther south by this time. All they'll want from you will be 'jaw-bone.' "

Scott suddenly realized that the old man had put his finger on the weak point in Jack's story. He spoke up quickly, to change the subject. "Next week," he blurted out, "Jack and I are making a trip into the mountains with Hunter Sam. Jack wants to do some hunting and I'm going to try my hand at prospecting."

Gee-gee shot a keen glance from one boy to the other. "Mighty fine idea," he boomed. "I'll let you have a couple o' horses. Oscar will do to pack your dunnage and grub. He's a bit ornery, but Scott knows how to handle him. You can have Mac and take turns riding. Come to think o' it, that buckskin called Bingo is pretty well broken to the saddle. Take him along—then you'll both be able to ride."

The boys thanked Gee-gee warmly as they left the lunch table and departed in different directions, each to his own job. It was nearly supper time before Jack had all his oufit packed up from the dock and arranged in the tent. He came strolling over to the woodpile with a brand new rifle in his hands. He motioned Scott to stop sawing.

"Listen!" he whispered. From the direction of the bunkhouse came the sound of familiar voices.

Scott peeked around the corner of the mess-house. "Gold Brick!" he announced. "He usually starts back for Handy Creek as soon as he's picked up his mail. But this time he's sitting on the porch of the bunkhouse, having a long rag chew with Gee-gee. I wonder what they're talking about. Remember how they used to hang around together on the *Chutine?*"

Jack shrugged. "I figure Gee-gee is just naturally talkative. He talked to us quite a lot too, didn't he?"

"Ye-s-s. But, remember how he acted at lunch when the mountain trip came up? Didn't it seem to you that he was a little too pleased at the idea of getting us out of the way for a few days?"

"I think Gee-gee has a heart of gold—even if he did make it plain that he doesn't think I'm very smart as a trader." Jack laughed. "Don't worry about what he's hashing over with Gold Brick. I've a hunch we're going to find out a lot of things before long. Meantime, I'm not going to pass up a chance to bring back a mountain sheep head. . . . Look at this." He pumped open the breech of his rifle to make sure the magazine was empty. His eyes seemed to reflect the glitter of the blue-black barrel. He patted the polished walnut stock affectionately. "It's a swell little gun—a two fifty, three thousand—only shoots an eighty grain bullet, but with a muzzle velocity of twenty-eight hundred, it should be just right for sheep at three hundred yards."

"Gosh!" Scott had a broad grin on his face. "You sound bloodthirsty! All I'll be armed with is my geologist's pick."

The next few days passed quickly enough. On the afternoon of the fourth day, Scott had the satisfaction of driving his ax into the worn chopping-block for the last time.

Next morning, the boys were up early, to find blue sky above them and the first rays of sunlight thrusting into the valley to burn the puffs of white mist off the hilltops. They loaded Oscar with their dunnage and kitchen boxes, Gee-gee working opposite Scott. The boy was taking up the last turn in the diamond-hitch when he heard Hunter Sam admiring Jack's rifle.

"That's nice gun. Too small for moose. But—sure, I find sheep for you. I'll take you up to the mountain with the wool on it."

Scott yanked the lash-rope tight and wheeled around. "You mean to say, Sam, there're so many sheep up there that the mountain looks as if it's covered with wool?"

The old Indian grunted. "I don't mean sheep wool—I mean wool that belongs to the mountain."

Scott didn't waste time asking another question. He thought he knew what the Indian meant: up above the tree line there must be grasses with flower heads that looked like cotton wool.

He swung into the saddle. His father called out, "Good hunting!" and they were on their way.

The horses plodded steadily along, following a trail that wound through the aspens and skirted the spruce groves close to the creek. Scott realized they formed an odd procession. Hunter Sam walked in front, leading his old cayuse, which carried a small pack. Scott was next, mounted on Mac, with Oscar's halter-rope looped over his saddle horn. Jack brought up the rear, jostling awkwardly on Bingo.

Dinty loped faithfully alongside Jack, but Manty seemed to be everywhere. He flushed grouse out of the thickets, chased snowshoe rabbits and barked at squirrels and anything else that moved. Scott kept calling him back, but the dog obeyed him reluctantly.

Hunter Sam shook his head and frowned. "Dog too

noisy—no good for hunting sheep."

Scott gritted his teeth and gave Manty another scolding. He wondered if he ever would be able to teach his dog to leave small animals alone.

It was well past noon when they came to the triangular flat where Handy Creek flowed into Osprey. As the boys dismounted stiffly, the old Indian announced, with a knowing look in his eyes, "Better we camp here tonight. We start up mountain tomorrow."

There were no protests. The horses were unsaddled and immediately had a good roll on the ground. After that they got up and cropped contentedly at the withered bunch grass and lupin amongst the alders.

The boys cut poles and erected the eight by ten tent. They had brought it along because the mosquito season was over and they could expect frosty nights in the mountains. They had brought a folding camp stove, but they didn't bother to set it up now. They cooked their meal over an open campfire.

They were ravenously hungry, so they made short work of the moose steaks, fried with onions, and potatoes roasted in the ashes. After they were through, Hunter Sam sat in front of the fire and puffed at his pipe.

Jack stood looking at him whimsically. "Solid comfort —eh? I don't mind admitting I'm more comfortable standing up than sitting down. Let's take a walk up the creek."

"Suits me." Scott was massaging his thighs. "I feel the same way."

Jack picked up his rifle and they started along a well defined trail. In muddy places close to the water there were clear imprints of caulked boots, with the caulks arranged in a series of diamond shapes.

Scott stooped to examine them. "Gold Brick, no doubt about it. Gold Brick! Everything about that man is flashy —right down to the pattern of his boot caulks."

There were other footprints in the mud—smooth and rounded. "Moccasins," Jack commented. "Those must be Tommy Naas's tracks. They look fresh, too." The two dogs trotted ahead of the boys with their noses to the ground, whining like vacuum cleaners.

Scott and Jack followed behind them for about half a mile until they came in sight of a low hill, topped with pines, that hid the next turn of the creek. Here Manty suddenly shot up the slope, barking in machine-gun bursts. Scott glimpsed a flash of his white paws and then Manty disappeared into the trees. Dinty, lumbering after the small dog, was still in sight.

Suddenly the sharp, earsplitting blast of a rifle shot splintered through the jack pines. Manty's barking stopped abruptly and Scott's heart turned over. He jumped off the trail and crouched behind a log beside Jack, who instantly pumped a shell into the breech of his rifle.

"Dinty! Here, boy! Come here!" Jack shouted—but Dinty galloped on into the pines.

Angry snarls came from the hill, mingled with the murmuring of a human voice. In a moment or two, the voice became an intelligible shout. "Hey! You down there! Make this big dog of yours leave me alone."

"All right—but no more funny business, or he'll fix you properly," Jack yelled in reply. Guided by Dinty's growls, he led the way cautiously up the hill, with his rifle at the ready.

Halfway up the knoll, Manty came dancing out of the bush, sniffed at Scott's feet and dashed off again. The boy felt he could almost cry with relief at finding his dog alive and unhurt.

As they struggled on up the hill, the underbrush thinned out. Suddenly, about twenty paces above them, they saw the figure of a man, cowering with his back against a tree. His rifle lay on the ground and Dinty crouched snarling in front of him. It was Tommy Naas!

Scott felt a hot flush of anger surge within him. "You . . . you tried to shoot my dog!"

"That's crazy talk!" Tommy kept his eyes on Dinty. "No Indian ever shoot bear dog. I just stop him from barking. Fire in the air and he go looking to find what I shot."

Jack took hold of Dinty's collar and scratched his ears. Then he unloaded his rifle and the three of them sat down.

"What were you doing here?" Jack asked bluntly.

"Hunting." Tommy Naas fumbled at a rawhide pouch slung on his belt. He pulled out a packet of tobacco and at the same time a small glass bottle rolled on the ground, followed by a fragment of something yellow and metallic.

Scott shot out his hand and grabbed the bottle and the yellow fragment. For a second or two he stared at them, his eyes blinking with surprise. Then, with a surly look, the Indian snatched them away from him.

Scott let them go without protest. "Gold Brick must be working rich ground up the creek. How's he going about it—shoveling-in or ground-sluicing?"

The corners of Tommy's mouth twitched downward. "I don't know anything about this mining business. All I know that's my wages—nuggets and high grade quartz." He rolled a cigaret and lit it.

Scott stretched out on the pine needles that carpeted the ground and studied Tommy's face. By golly! It did look like the one he'd glimpsed in the tank at Telegraph Creek.

"Now I know where I first saw you, Tommy," Scott said. "It was at Telegraph Creek. You went down the trail while Jack and I were cleaning out the water tank."

Tommy scowled. "I don't remember," he grunted.

Scott persisted. "I think I'm right. It was just after the wagons were loaded. Weren't you in town that night?"

Tommy's eyes narrowed as he took a long draw at his cigaret. "How should I know? That's long time ago."

"Well, maybe I'm wrong." Scott got up. "See you later, Tommy."

"Where you headed for?" the Indian asked uneasily.

"Up to Pyramid Mountain with Hunter Sam," Scott answered. Manty was at his heels and Jack, with Dinty, followed him down to the creek.

Scott could hardly wait until they reached the bottom of the slope. His voice trembled with excitement as he spoke. "I thought I'd see what he had to say. I didn't get a good enough look at that reflection in the tank to be sure. But did you notice how worried he seemed to get? And he hasn't got any more of an alibi about that Norse knife than Gee-gee has."

"That doesn't prove anything though, does it?" Jack pointed out.

"Maybe not. But what would you say if I told you the gold in the bottle was Osprey Creek gold? And that yellow stuff Tommy called quartz was a piece of pyrites from my rock samples?"

Jack stared at him incredulously. "You're sure? Could you swear to it?"

"Well, of course, just getting a quick look like that, no one could be absolutely certain. But there're no pyrites near here and I should remember what my samples looked like. And I should know Osprey Creek gold by now." Scott nodded at the blue water of Handy Creek. "Mighty clear water, Jack! Doesn't look as though Gold Brick is doing any sluicing, does it? Say! Instead of climbing the mountain tomorrow, let's pay him a visit and find out what goes on."

Jack shook his head. "Not after telling Tommy Naas we were going to Pyramid Mountain. I miss my guess if he wasn't snooping around to see what we're up to. If we go on up the mountain, it should put them off their guard and we may have a good chance of finding out something on our way back."

Scott felt that he couldn't find fault with Jack's logic.

16

"WOLVERINE!"

TOMMY NAAS . . . I'm almost sure those nuggets he
has are from Osprey Creek . . . and the fool's gold must
be from my missing rock samples. Tommy camped up
Handy Creek with Gold Brick . . . no sign of them
doing any mining . . . and we're getting farther and
farther away from them. So ran Scott's thoughts the next
morning as they plodded up the lower slopes of Pyramid
Mountain.

But he had more immediate problems to worry about.
He was continuously ducking his head close to Mac's neck
to avoid the low branches that overhung the trail. He
had to grip the reins tight when the horse struggled for
a foothold in loose rubble or plunged headlong into steep
gullies. Every once in a while he would catch sight of Jack
and his friend's confident face gave him encouragement.

He had to admit that Jack must have the right idea. If
they carried on with this trip, Gold Brick and Tommy
would have no reason to believe that the boys suspected
them. He and Jack would have a chance to catch them off

guard on the way back.

"Oh, my aching back!" Jack groaned as they dismounted to lead the horses through a maze of windfalls. "This is a tough climb, but I'm going to get that mountain sheep head in spite of . . . in spite of Gold Brick and Tommy and high water!"

Scott remembered why he had longed all summer to explore the mountains. It hadn't been to spy on Gold Brick—it had been to look for the Mother Lode. He must keep his eyes open, he told himself. But how would he go about his prospecting? There was such an enormous expanse of country to cover. Sometimes, when they came to an open ridge, he could see bare rock peaks towering on every hand and the tree-covered slopes below faded into the distance as far as eye could see.

At last, Hunter Sam tugged at the bridle of his old cayuse and grunted, "Here good place for camp tonight, I guess."

Saddle-sore and weary, Scott unlashed Oscar's packs and set out with the ax to cut some tent poles. He noticed that the pine and spruce had dwindled to scattered clumps. Twilight was falling and he could see only the wedge shape of an occasional twisted balsam fir between their campsite and the rocky crags of Pyramid Mountain. They had reached the edge of the tree line! Scott remembered from the maps that this would mean they had climbed close to the six-thousand-foot level.

"Look in the serpentine rock; that's where nature has hidden her treasures. Perhaps it's the Mother Lode; perhaps it's something more valuable." The memory of Lars's words was clear in Scott's mind. He knew what to do now. Tomorrow he would prospect in the serpentine.

So, next morning, when Hunter Sam and Jack had packed their lunches and prepared to start out on foot for the sheep pastures on the higher levels, Scott spoke up eagerly when the Indian said, "Have to tie up dogs —no good for hunt sheep. Scare 'em all away."

"I'll stay around camp and keep an eye on them," he offered.

The sun had just risen to make the steep rock escarpments above shine like black glass. Here and there in the distance, Scott saw patches of white dotted on the mountainside. "Sam," he asked, "is that snow?"

"No! That's what I tell you about. That's 'wool that belongs mountain.' Over that ridge there's lots of wool. Not far—maybe about mile—you go see if you like."

"You bet! This I'll have to see." Scott's mind was seething with curiosity. His guess when Sam had first mentioned 'wool that belongs mountain' had been wrong. There couldn't be flowers or grass up there on the bald rock. The white patches must be outcroppings of rock, and yet, even in the distance, they looked like wool, just as Sam said.

"You take care of yourself, fellow," Jack warned.

"Don't worry!" Scott laughed. "Manty will look after me."

The boy stood in front of the tent, holding Dinty by the collar, until the hunters had disappeared among the crags. Then, with the dogs at his heels, he plodded up out of the trees and started to climb a hog-back of bare rock in the direction that Sam had indicated.

At the crest of the ridge, Scott caught his breath. A few hundred yards below him lay acres of the white "wool." "Come on, boys," he called to the dogs. "We'll soon find out about this 'wool that belongs mountain.' " Slipping and sliding, he started off at an angle down a steep slope that was strewn with dark green boulders. He stopped to examine one of them.

"By Jimminy! This fits the description in Dad's book." He recited from memory, " 'Blackish green, merging into brownish and other colors, feels smooth and somewhat greasy.' " There was no doubt about it—this was the serpentine rock.

Minutes later, he was standing ankle-deep in the "wool." Now he could understand what Sam meant. It really did belong to the mountain. It was part of the greenish rock, split and shredded by frost and sun into millions of thin white fibres. At close quarters, the surface appeared gray and weathered, but he scooped up handfuls that were snow white. He found splintered fragments of the rock which fractured easily along straight lines of cleavage when he tapped them with his pick.

Scott took up one of the samples he had broken off. It glittered dark green and golden in the sunlight, but it shredded to delicate fibres of pure white between his fingers. He struck a match and held some of the fine threads in the flame. They twisted and curled upward but remained unchanged by the heat.

"For Pete's sake!" he gasped. "Asbestos! That's what it is. Asbestos isn't valuable like gold, but there's such a heck of a lot of it here . . . I wonder. . . ."

The boy looked around him for a few minutes. "Well," he decided finally, "I suppose the thing to do is to make a map so I can prove there really is a big deposit here."

Remembering the "journey" he had made when he passed his First Class Scout tests, he took rough bearings from the most prominent mountain peaks. And then he started to pace. He estimated the white strip on the mountainside averaged about two hundred feet in width. Then he scrambled along to where the showing ended in solid rock and from there he paced carefully back in the direction of the camp. The westering sun was low on the horizon when he climbed back over the hog-back and headed toward the timber.

Scott sat down at the foot of a balsam fir to complete his map. "Two thousand feet long," he said to himself, "probably more. I'll bet my paces are longer now than when I took my Scouting tests this spring."

Dinty sniffed around impatiently and loped off toward the camp, but Manty stayed, ranging around in the dwarf willows at the edge of the trees. Suddenly he let out a shrill *"yip"* and a blur of white forms whirred out of the brush.

"Good grief! Ptarmigan—now you have something new to bark at. Come back, Manty!" Scott noticed a sun-bleached moose antler lying a few yards away. He went over and picked it up and tapped it against tree. "Come back! Come here, Manty!" he yelled.

The effect was magical. The dog was at his side instantly,

head up and tail wagging. Scott went on sketching with one hand and tapping the moose horn against the tree with the other.

It took less than five minutes to complete his notes. He was putting his pencil in his pocket when Manty snarled a warning. The dog's hackles suddenly bristled and he stood with every muscle in his body trembling.

Scott's heart skipped a beat. He looked around and caught a blurred glimpse of the long, ugly face of a bull moose, huge flat antlers swaying to and fro above dilated nostrils.

Jimmy Brokenose's words on the trail flashed through his mind: "In the fall, they don't always run away."

The moose gave an angry, coughing grunt and charged straight at Scott. The boy tried to force his rubbery legs to move. Get behind the tree . . . my only chance . . . not a tree in sight high enough to climb . . . but I may be able to hide behind one . . ."

Then Manty was suddenly in the path of the huge animal. Bursting into a frenzied volley of barking, the tiny dog nipped at the creature's heels. The moose reared up and stabbed down at Manty with its front hoofs, but the dog sprang nimbly out of the way. The bull snorted, wheeled sharply and crashed off through the brush.

"Whew! Good dog, Manty! Th-thanks a l-lot!" Scott was still trembling as he headed for the tent. But he soon recovered from his experience as he became absorbed in the job of lighting the fire and mixing up some baking powder bannock.

It was quite dark by the time the hunters returned.

Dinty's tail waved happily as Jack sat down on the sleeping boughs beside him.

Hunter Sam's face was impassive, but Jack looked a little uncomfortable when Scott questioned him. "Well, was it a record head?"

"Let's face it," Jack said humbly. "That big ram was standing there on the sky-line. His neck didn't look thick enough to hold up those long spiral horns. It was a perfect setup, but . . . I got buck fever and missed. I'm glad, though, the only way I want to hunt anything as beautiful as that is with a camera."

Scott secretly agreed with him, but he couldn't resist ribbing his friend a little. "Some hunter you are. What did you buy that rifle for—to shoot squirrels?"

"Phooey on squirrels! On the way back I shot a moose." Then Jack added defensively, "But that was different, it's fresh meat for the mine." He grinned. "Besides, I had to prove to Sam that my rifle isn't too light for moose."

"*Skookum* rifle—*hi-yu* fat meat, too," Hunter Sam admitted. "We make cache with small trees to keep meat away from coyotes. Tomorrow we pack back to mine."

"Heck! I could have killed a moose myself, if I'd had a gun." Scott burst out with his own moose story.

The Indian shook his head as he listened to the boy's account of his adventure. "That's bad thing. This time of year moose look for mate. You know what he think? He hear horn hitting tree. He say, 'That's another bull moose—he look for trouble. I go fight him.' Lucky thing you have bear dog with you."

Scott could understand now. "Gee," he mumbled, "and

I thought banging on a tree would scare a moose away!"

A few minutes later he was wrapped up in his sleeping bag and the knowledge that Manty was curled up at his feet made him feel contented. And trying to guess the value of the "wool" he had found on the mountainside soon put him to sleep.

Early next morning, they broke camp and took the horses into the stunted timber to pick up the moose meat. As they neared the scene of the cache, it was clear that something was amiss. The meat was scattered around on the ground in all directions. The boys stared in astonishment at a hindquarter that had been dragged a hundred yards from the cache. It was as much as the two of them together could lift.

Jack gasped, "This meat stinks! I—I think I'm going to be sick!"

"Me, too!" Scott stepped back. "Phew!"

"Wolverine!" Scott wheeled around at the sound of Hunter Sam's voice. He was startled at the anger smouldering in the Indian's dark eyes.

"Wolverine! He do this!" Sam growled through clenched teeth. "That's why old-time Indians call him the devil. He don't care for eat—just to make mischief. All this good meat he cover with musk—nothing eat it now —not even foxes!"

The Indian moved silently over to his cayuse and inspected the contents of his saddlebags. Then he turned to the boys.

"I make hunt for moose by myself. I show you fellows easy trail down to the valley." The ghost of a smile wrinkled across Sam's weather-beaten face. "Three horses, two dogs—you couldn't get lost. You want to try it?"

The boys exchanged glances and chorused, "Sure we do!"

Hunter Sam didn't look back when they led the horses away from the ruined cache. His last warning as the boys started down the new trail was, "If you ever meet wolverine—remember he is devil. You shoot him!"

17

SCOTT AND JACK PLAN TO SOLVE A MYSTERY

THE boys were starting to make camp on the banks of the upper reaches of Osprey Creek. Jack smiled as he unstrapped the leather rifle-boot from his saddle. "Didn't need a rifle, did we?"

"I'll say we didn't!" Scott agreed. "We didn't see anything bigger than a snowshoe rabbit!"

All day the horses had clip-clopped down a winding trail through evergreen forests, and now they had come to flats covered with aspen. The setting sun was turning the frost-tinted leaves to orange and gold.

"Sort of creepy, just the same," Jack murmured, "all those stories about wolverine following trappers around their lines."

"Forget it!" Scott shrugged. "We're not trappers."

Jack didn't answer until they had the tent pitched and a fire kindled in the stove. He opened a can of pork and beans and warmed them in the frying pan. "We're not hunters either," he said wryly. "But you're a sure enough prospector, Scott. That asbestos you located sounds like the real McCoy to me. I never could see what use gold is —we don't even have gold money any more. But think of the things asbestos is used for! Brake-lining, fireproof shingles, insulation for furnaces and refrigerators . . . hundreds of other things."

"Don't forget you'll be in on it, too, if it does turn out to be worth anything. There's lots of it and I'll have Dad stake a claim in your name. It will be a long time, though, before any of us makes anything out of it—it's so hard to get at. Besides," Scott pointed out, "I don't even know if it's the type that can be used commercially."

"You'll find out, though," Jack said. "That's the sort of thing you'll learn at University."

"If I ever get there." Scott's brow wrinkled. "It all depends on how the mine pays in the next few weeks. Dad doesn't say much, but I have a hunch he's disappointed at the amount of gold we're getting. Darn it all! I'd feel a lot better if we knew just what Gold Brick and Tommy Naas are up to."

Jack got up and started to unroll his sleeping bag. He stifled a yawn as he suggested, "Let's quit worrying and turn in now. We'll be at Handy Creek tomorrow afternoon; then we'll figure out what to do about Gold Brick and Tommy."

"It's a deal," muttered Scott drowzily as he rolled up in his eiderdown.

The next morning dawned cold and gray across a threatening sky. Scott kept a tight rein as he swung into the saddle, for the nip in the air was making Mac frisk and prance. The boys headed down the creek, and by the time the horses had quietened down, Scott looked about him to find that all signs of a trail had vanished. Sticks of driftwood and tangles of uprooted brush were stacked up in confused piles on the flats all around them.

He called out, "We must be upstream from where the slide was. The water has been backed up over the trail here."

"This is worse than devil's-club!" Jack exclaimed as he rode up alongside Scott. "Makes a fellow feel completely lost. I sure had a pipe dream when I expected to find gold in these creeks. I wouldn't know where to start. I guess I can forget about sending extra money home to my sister."

Scott winced at the note of discouragement in his friend's voice. "You never can tell," he said, trying to sound cheerful. They wandered aimlessly around among the driftwood for almost half an hour and then Scott pointed to a knoll downstream and shouted, "Look! There's a trail leading up into the jack pine."

They guided their horses around the debris caught in the clumps of willows and alders on the flats and headed up the knoll. Soon they were looking down at the white-rippled stream, curving sharply back from a steep clay cut-bank. The horses plodded softly on a thick carpet of pine needles. Scott heard the thunder of rushing water, growing gradually louder until it drowned out the jingle of the bits and the creak of saddle leather.

He looked back and called to Jack, "We're up above the canyon." When he looked ahead again, he yanked instinctively at the reins, but Mac had already come to a dead stop. In front of him, the trail ended abruptly at a jagged edge of rock.

The boys dismounted and advanced cautiously toward the rim where uprooted pines were hanging, with wilting boughs pointing down to a fresh scar in the solid rock of the canyon wall. A hundred feet below, the creek cascaded in white foam over a jumble of rock which appeared as vague black shapes beneath the water.

Scott stood stroking the back of his head. "Now we know what cut off the water last month. But I can't figure it out. I could understand if that clay bank on the other side had started a big slide. But there's something darned queer about a big chunk breaking off this rock cliff."

"Just one of those things, I suppose." Jack shrugged his shoulders. "Looks like our only course now is to lead the horses around the bluff and pick up the trail on the other side of the slide."

The horses walked with uneven, jerky steps as they headed into the pines. Scott felt a sharp tug at the reins as Mac shied unaccountably at a juniper thicket. He noticed that all three horses had their heads up, with their ears twitching and their nostrils dilated.

"Here, Dinty! Come back, boy!" Jack was struggling to control Bingo with one hand while he drew his rifle from its boot with the other. He yelled, "Must be a bear! Horses stampede at bear scent!"

"Manty! Manty!" Scott shouted as he tried to hold his plunging horse. But both dogs disappeared into the brush.

A machine-gun volley of Manty's shrill yelps came from not far away. The sharp note of urgency sent a chill up Scott's spine.

Dinty's deep-throated roar burst forth and suddenly ended in a sickening scream.

At the sound, Mac reared up so violently that Scott felt his hands seared by the reins and he was thrown to the ground. The horse dashed on by him. He had no chance of stopping the other two horses as they thundered past, with their ears flat, each urged on by the other's panic-stricken neighing.

Scott stumbled after Jack, who was running, rifle in hand, in the direction of Manty's frantic barking. Within seconds they came upon Dinty. An animal, only half his size, had the old dog by the side of the neck. His legs were thrashing frantically. Jack raised his gun to his shoulder, but Scott yelled, "Don't shoot! You can't help hitting Dinty if you do!"

Desperately, the boy ripped a dead branch off a tree and struck at the animal's bear-like muzzle. It hissed and twisted toward him, its body moving like a snake. And in that split-second Scott smelt the same sickening stench of musk that had hung over Hunter Sam's ruined cache. The Indian's words spurred him to action. "Wolverine! He is a devil!"

Scott lashed out with his club and missed. The creature had evidently aimed at Dinty's jugular vein, but some sudden movement of the dog had deflected its aim. Now it was waiting its time to loosen its grip momentarily and make a fresh try at the fast-weakening old dog. Just then Manty dashed in front of his master. The wolverine crouched and lunged at the little dog with a weaving, shuffling gait. But the bear dog was behind it, nipping at its flanks.

The boy heard the wolverine's jaws click as it whirled and snapped at thin air where Manty had been a fraction of a second before. And then the long, brown, furry body, with bright yellow flanks, retreated into the brush.

"Son of a gun!" Jack grunted. "They say he's not afraid of anything from a grizzly down, but he's too crafty to face a man at close quarters!"

"Come on!" Scott ran back toward the canyon at the sound of two sharp yelps from Manty.

They came upon the dog, whining under his breath, staring up into the branches of a tall pine tree that slanted outward over the canyon wall. At first, as the boys peered up into the green boughs, they saw nothing. But, after a moment or two, the wolverine's light-colored flanks gave him away and they spotted him, clinging close to the top of the tree.

Jack stepped back, pumped a cartridge into the breech, lifted his rifle and took careful aim. At the sharp crack as he squeezed the trigger, the boys saw the long, flat paws, like those of a cub bear, clutch convulsively at the tree trunk. Then the furry body crashed from branch to branch, hurtled out into space and plummeted into the canyon.

Manty gave one sharp woof of defiance as it disappeared. Scott scratched the dog's head affectionately. "Good boy! If it hadn't been for you, the wolverine would have put an end to Dinty and then got away to spoil more of Hunter Sam's meat and to rob his trap line in the winter."

The boys hurried back up the slope to Dinty. The old dog had struggled to his feet. He had a nasty gash on his neck but he wagged his tail valiantly.

Scott swallowed hard and his eyes blinked back tears of which he was not ashamed. Jack muttered in a husky voice, "It's tough, old boy, but we'll just take it easy going back and you'll be all right, thanks to Manty."

Scott turned up the collar of his jacket as he felt a cold drizzle starting to fall from the ashen skies. "Suppose we'd better hit the trail," he said. "The horses will high-tail it back to the mine. We have about twenty miles to hike, so we won't crawl in until after dark. We're going to be plenty cold and hungry before we get there." He suddenly let out a yell. "Hey, look at this!" He crouched over, staring at a patch of clay in the shade of a tree which had protected it from the rain. In it there was the imprint of diamond-patterned boot-caulks!

"Gold Brick was up here! A few weeks ago, by the looks of his tracks. I wonder what he was up to?" Jack puzzled.

They didn't have to look far for the answer. A few yards away, there was an uneven pile of flat slabs of rock.

Scott exclaimed, "It's some sort of a cache. Look! The wolverine must have been clawing some of the rocks off the top when Dinty surprised him."

It took all the strength the boys could muster to pull back another slab, which was no bigger than the one the wolverine had already moved. Now they could see what was hidden in the cache—a stout wooden box marked DYNAMITE!

Jack let out a whoop. "Wolverine—carcajou—skunk-bear—devil—whatever they call you, your habits have put us on the right track. This means that Gold Brick must have blasted off a piece of the cliff to stop the water power at the mine."

Inside Scott's mind all the pieces of the puzzle seemed to be fitting together now. Gold Brick had caused the rock slide. It was the same sort of thing that had happened to the Jack o' Diamonds. Gold Brick had hoped to slow down the working of the mine so that Scott's father would want to sell out.

Surely the cat had been deliberately wrecked for the same reason. Scott couldn't believe that Gee-gee had anything to do with that. In spite of Gold Brick's alibi, he felt that Tommy Naas must have been acting as a stooge for Gold Brick, if the Indian had cut the brake-rope.

What about the wreck of the boat in the rapids? A picture flashed across Scott's mind of Gold Brick, with a water pail in his hand, walking up from the lake in the dead of night. How stupid he had been never to have given it a thought before! It was a fairly safe guess that Gold Brick had been putting water in Antoin's gas.

Then there was the question of the not overbright Tommy Naas with iron pyrites that he thought were rich quartz, and with nuggets that looked like Osprey Creek gold. Probably Gold Brick had stolen Scott's rock samples at Wrangell, thinking they had something to do with the mine. And it didn't seem hard to believe that he had been coming down at dawn, before the first shift went to work, to steal the biggest nuggets from the sluices.

Scott looked at his companion with excitement burning his eyes. "We've really got the goods on Gold Brick now. Let's head up Handy Creek and have a showdown with him."

Jack shook his head. "I don't think that would do us much good. He's crafty like a wolverine. Remember Hunter Sam telling us how they steal animals from the traps and carry them off a short distance and bury them in the snow? That's Gold Brick for you, I'll bet—I mean your rock samples and the gold wouldn't be sitting on the table if you walked into his cabin. What we've got to do is catch him red-handed."

"Uh-huh. Guess you're right." Scott was silent for several minutes. There were a lot of things to consider. They could go straight back to the mine and persuade his father to post watchmen at the sluices. But if they did that and their suspicions turned out to be false, they would feel like fools for crying: "Wolf." How much more satisfying it would be, if they could solve the problem by themselves.

Scott wondered about the horses and decided they would plod slowly along the trail after they reached the level of the creek and the scent of wolverine vanished. Late in the evening, they should be grazing with the other horses in the meadow upstream from the mine. They probably wouldn't be discovered until after breakfast tomorrow.

While Scott was pondering these questions, Manty had flushed a grouse and was "woofing" softly under the tree where the terrified bird sat with its neck outstretched. Jack rested his rifle on another tree and its sharp report rippled through the trees—but his shot missed.

"Shoots high at this range," he grunted. And then, taking a fine bead, he fired again and the bird fluttered to the ground with its head severed. "Hah!" he exclaimed triumphantly. "We'll eat, after all."

"Sure!" There was confidence in Scott's voice as his words poured out. "Manty will find more grouse and there will be blueberries down by the creek. I figure Gold Brick will be lying low until we get back from the mountains. He'll see the tracks of our horses on the trail this evening and light out for the sluices at dawn tomorrow."

"Could be," Jack ventured cautiously.

Scott's voice rose with excitement. "Don't you see? It's our chance to work this thing out. We can circle off the trail before we get to Handy Creek. There's a small stream where we can cross back and climb up onto the terraces without leaving any tracks. We can build a wickiup and tough it out around a campfire for the night. At dawn, I'll be hiding below the tailing dump and you can be up at the dam. If Gold Brick is doing any high-grading, we'll catch him—going or coming."

This time there was nothing cautious about Jack's reply. "Come on then," he said tersely. "What are we waiting for?"

18

A THIEF UNMASKED

"L-LIE d-down, M-manty!" Scott ordered in a low voice. The pre-dawn chill made his teeth chatter as he crouched on the wet gravel below the lower section of the sluice-boxes.

Manty obeyed instantly. Scott thought: He seems to have grown up since his brush with the bull moose and the wolverine.

A faint tinge of gold was edging the broken clouds overhead. Scott looked at his watch. "Half an hour gone already," he said to himself. "Wish I could be sure that Jack found his way up to the dam in the dark. No sign of Gold Brick. Perhaps we're on a wild goose chase. It'll be daylight soon."

Suddenly Manty was on his feet. He sniffed the air and pricked up his ears. Scott held up a warning finger. "S-s-sh!" The dog froze, stiff-legged, motionless except for the nervous quivering of his short, bushy tail, which stood up like a big shaving brush. It was several minutes before the boy's ears detected the crunch of footsteps on the gravel at the far end of the sluice.

"Click . . . clack . . . crunch," and then a pause. In a few seconds they would start again, always coming closer. Scott's heart turned over and started to thump. Somebody was walking slowly along the sluice-boxes. It must be Gold Brick! But where was Jack? He had said that he would fasten Dinty near the dam with a length of rope that he had found beside the cache and come on alone because the big dog might make too much noise. Besides, Dinty was still feeling the effects of his encounter with the wolverine.

Had Jack missed the trail to the dam? If he hadn't, he should be appearing at any moment now, with his rifle pointed at Gold Brick, saying, "All right, Schnider, put 'em up! We've got you at last!"

But the footsteps came closer and closer until they reached the last section of the sluice. The box was raised a foot or so above the gravel. Scott peered underneath it and recognized Gold Brick's high leather boots.

Still no sign of Jack! Gold Brick was moving very slowly now because it was in the riffles of this box that most of the "clean-up" was concentrated. Near-panic gripped Scott as he signaled frantically for Manty to keep back. The dog's every muscle was trembling with pent-up energy. Scott realized that Gold Brick would be sure to see them after a few more steps.

Something must have happened to Jack! Scott knew he couldn't tackle Gold Brick singlehanded. He jumped to his feet and ran toward the tailing dump. Out of the corner of his eye, he caught a glimpse of Gold Brick vaulting over the sluice-box. Manty exploded into a frenzy of barking behind him. Scott could guess that he was snapping at Schnider's heels, but his sharp teeth wouldn't be able to penetrate the heavy leather boots.

Scott heard the heavy crunch of those boots close behind him as he neared the top of the dump. Gold Brick, with his longer strides, was gaining on him. The boy's thoughts kept time with his heaving lungs. "A few more yards . . . then down-hill. . . . I'll really be able to sprint on the trail. . . . He won't dare to follow me much closer to the mine. . . ."

He was nearly on solid ground when his foot slipped on a loose rock. Before he could get up, Gold Brick grabbed the throat of his shirt and twisted it until the boy choked for breath. Scott drove his fist into the man's flabby jowl —it felt like a punching bag. He kicked savagely in rapid succession—but his foot bounced back from the leather-clad shins. Then he felt stubby fingers wrapped around one of his wrists. His arm was twisted behind his back. He gasped with pain as he was forced to his knees.

"So! Doing a little snooping, huh? I never could stand nosey kids. Suppose you happened to fall into the creek . . . you'd get drowned, wouldn't you?" Gold Brick gloated as he held Scott helpless.

But all the while, Manty was dashing back and forth and nipping at the man's heels. Gold Brick hooked a vicious backward kick and sent the dog flying. Scott twisted his head toward the dog. He was filled with a blind fury as he heard Manty's yelp of pain. But something he saw in the distance gave him new hope. A figure was running along the sluices toward the lower monitor. Jack had arrived at last!

It was a question of stalling for time now. "Go ahead and throw me in," Scott muttered. "I can swim like a fish. *You* should know that. You had one try at drowning me in the rapids."

"So what?" Gold Brick snarled. "Just because you saw me around Antoin's boat doesn't prove I put water in the gas. Anyway, you won't be telling about it. If you're found in the creek with your head bashed in, people will think you hit your head on a rock when you fell in."

Before Scott had time to digest the full implication of Gold Brick's words, Manty had recovered enough to return to the fray. A furry bundle of fury leapt at Scott's tormentor and needle-sharp teeth clamped on Gold Brick's wrist.

Startled, the man relaxed his grip. Scott wrenched himself free and sprinted back toward the sluice-boxes. Only a second or two head start . . . beat of heavy feet pounding behind him again . . . a blurred picture of Jack coming toward him . . . no rifle in his hand! Gold Brick too close now . . . Jack can't use the rifle!

Then there was a terrific swoosh and a wall of icy spray carried Scott off his feet. Everything seemed hazy for a few seconds. Then Scott picked himself up and saw Gold Brick, writhing and cursing as he lay on the ground in the full force of the hydraulic jet. After a minute or two, Jack turned the stream to one side and rushed down, shouting to Scott, "Grab his feet before he can get up."

Gold Brick, battered and bruised, and with his wind

nearly knocked out, still had fight left in him. Scott clung desperately to the kicking legs, while Jack flung himself onto the man's chest and struggled to pinion his flailing arms.

"Maybe I'll have to give you the water treatment again," Jack grunted. Gold Brick answered with a string of oaths. Just then Scott heard footsteps running toward them.

"All right, you ornery coyote! We've got you at last!"

At the sound of the words, Scott looked up to see Gee-gee standing over them, with "Old Betsy" in his hand. Beside the old man was the khaki-clad figure of Constable Black.

"Get up!" the constable said tersely to Gold Brick. "You'll have to come with me and answer some questions."

The policeman didn't even draw his revolver, but, to Scott's amazement, Gold Brick struggled to his feet and followed without a word.

As the pair started toward the mine, the constable snapped, "Put that gun away, Gee-gee. I suppose you've forgotten to get a permit for it, the same as you forget to get a hunting license and a license for your pack-train."

Scott couldn't help grinning. "For Pete's sake! Is that why you have a bad name with the police?" he asked Gee-gee. The old man looked away sheepishly, rumbling, "Danged if there was all this red tape about a gun in the old days." Then, suddenly, he was his old self again. "My wrangler found your horses in the meadow this mornin'. Oscar hadn't lost his pack, so I told your dad nothing very terrible could have happened. Just the same, he's

mighty worried. We'd better get going. He's just getting
ready to start out and look for you."

Scott didn't have a very clear recollection of what happened during the ensuing few hours. He remembered his
father reverently exclaiming, "Thank God, you're safe,
Son!" as he staggered, cold and exhausted, into the bed-
room behind the office. Then he had a faint memory of
rolling up between heavy woollen blankets and sipping a
hot drink made from powdered milk with a dash of something in it that tasted like brown sugar. It tickled his nose
and made him choke, but after he got it down, he felt
deliciously warm inside and he must have gone right to
sleep.

Late in the afternoon, Scott was awakened by the
murmur of voices on the other side of the door. His
muscles felt stiff and sore, especially his right shoulder,
but there didn't seem to be anything seriously wrong. He
pulled on his clothes and slipped into the office.

His father was sitting with his arms folded, looking
grim and thoughtful. Jack's eyes flashed him a smile
from across the room. Gold Brick was standing in front
of the desk. Sitting on the other side, Constable Black
looked up and nodded. "Schnider was just telling us that
your dog attacked him, so he pretended he was going
to duck you in the creek, just for a gag."

"Hah! Hah! You could take it, though, couldn't you,
Scotty?" Gold Brick turned toward him with a smile
that Scott didn't return. "You boys had the last laugh.
Using the monitor like that! That was a good one on

me. Ho! Ho!"

Gold Brick had evidently recovered his self-confidence. "I was sorry about that rock slide—should have mentioned it before, I suppose. I was prospecting a quartz vein and used a little too much powder. Just one of those things that happen in the mining game."

The constable commented dryly, "Especially when you don't have a permit to use dynamite."

Before Gold Brick could reply, the door burst open and Tommy Naas shuffled in, looking sullen and frightened. Gee-gee strutted behind him, his right hand resting lightly on the ivory butt of his gun. Scott flashed a quick smile at Jack—it appeared that the matter of permits and licenses had been straightened out.

"No sign of any minin' up on Handy Creek," Gee-gee boomed, "but Tommy here was most co-operative. These here were cached under the woodpile." He set two small canvas sacks on the desk with a clunk.

The constable reached for the shallow sorting scoop and poured the contents of the smaller sack into it. Scott sucked in his breath as a stream of golden nuggets clattered against the copper pan. He was sure it was Osprey Creek gold now—but how could anyone prove it?

Gold Brick spoke as smoothly as ever. "Almost think it was from Osprey, wouldn't you? It happens that way sometimes. But this gold came from a rich pocket we struck on the other side of the pass."

"Interesting." The constable peered into the other bag. "What's this?" He scooped out a handful of rock fragments and spread them on the desk.

Gee-gee snorted, "Just plain rock!"

But there were no doubts in Scott's mind. "My rock samples!" he exclaimed as he walked over to the desk. "They disappeared from my bag at Wrangell. Let's see . . . obsidian . . . granite . . . porphyry . . . mica schist . . . they all seem to be here except some pieces of iron pyrites—fool's gold. Tommy has them; he thinks it's gold quartz!"

Hatred burned in the Indian's eyes as he glared at Gold Brick. "So! That's it—you think you make fool of me. Now it's my turn. I tell these people we never used pick or shovel all summer."

Schnider's pudgy jowls quivered. "Tommy's a good hand with horses, but he doesn't know much about prospecting. He never did catch on that I was panning out nuggets while he was away hunting."

"How about my rock samples?" Scott challenged.

Gold Brick tried to grin. "That's the funniest one yet. They must have fallen out of your bag on the dock at Wrangell. I picked them up but didn't say anything about them because they didn't seem to be of any value. You've got the laugh on me again, Scotty."

But Scott didn't even smile. He didn't believe a word Schnider was saying. He was staring at the knife lying on the desk. That must be the Norse knife Gold Brick had been carrying. Its pointed, double-edged blade, was only about three inches long. He remembered Jack telling him how these knives were made from soft metal, with narrow strips of hard steel welded along the edges.

A good grade of steel? That's what Gold Brick had told

Jack—but Gold Brick wasn't that dumb. He knew better than that. Jack had seen Schnider pick the knife up— but how did Jack know that it had been there all night?

Scott broke the electric silence that had held the occupants of the office in suspense. Looking squarely at Gold Brick, he asked, "Is this the knife Jack saw you put into your box when you came into the store on the morning the cat-train left?"

The bluff worked and Gold Brick stepped into the trap. "What of it?" he snarled. "I wasn't the only one who had a Norse knife!"

"But you were the only one who tried to conceal the fact it was in your possession." Constable Black's voice had a steel edge to it. "I have proof that the brake-rope was cut with one of these knives. You're getting in deeper all the time, Schnider. It will go easier with you if you tell us the whole story."

Gold Brick started to wilt like a leaky balloon. "All right! I cut the brake-rope and I put water in the gas at the lake. But all I wanted to do was slow down the freight so Haliburton would be in a mood to talk things over. I didn't mean anyone to get hurt. It was a business . . ."

The constable interrupted him. "Business!" he said grimly. "It sounds even worse than the Jack o' Diamonds affair. Well, we couldn't prove you had anything to do with that. But you seem to have overplayed your hand this time."

Gold Brick stared sheepishly at the gold on the desk.

"I needed something to show the big shots outside before they'd put up the money. I used to come down early in the mornings and pick out the biggest nuggets from the sluices.

"But I was keeping track of them." He turned a cringing look at Mr. Haliburton. "They would have been added to the price of the mine when you decided to sell out. There would have been money in it for both of us if I could have swung the deal. Those fellows could afford . . ." Gold Brick seemed to crumple under Dave Haliburton's frigid expression. "The rock samples . . . I borrowed them because I thought there'd be some nuggets among them. If Tim Donovan hadn't butted in when the *Chutine* was unloading, I'd have got them back into Scott's dunnage bag."

Gold Brick's eyes smoldered as his gaze shifted to Jack and then to Scott. "If it hadn't been for you and your side-kick, I'd have shown your father how to make some real money out of this mine," he snarled.

The constable looked at him with loathing. "That's enough! You'll have a chance to tell the rest to the magistrate when I get you into town. Gee-gee! Take him away and lock him up in the blacksmith shop."

Tommy Naas shifted uneasily on his feet. "You want me to take horses back?" he mumbled.

The constable nodded.

"Soon as snow flies," the Indian said anxiously, "I figure to go back to my own people on Naas River."

The constable leaned back in his chair and smiled.

"That's the smartest idea you've had since you came up north. You've always been in hot water in this country. You're only getting out of this mix-up by the skin of your teeth."

As the Indian padded out, Scott said to himself : I knew it all along. Tommy was just a stooge—that's all!

Mr. Haliburton went to the gold scales and started to weigh the nuggets. It was so quiet in the room that Scott could hear the tiny weights, that represented grains and half-grains, clink as they hit the brass pan. At last the weights exactly balanced the nuggets in the opposite pan —the beam stayed horizontal with scarcely a quiver.

Dave Haliburton made some pencil calculations on a note pad. "Just under a thousand dollars' worth," he announced. "I'll have this lot assayed separately and split the cheque between the two of you."

"Heck!" Jack's lips quivered. "I wasn't expecting . . ."

Mr. Haliburton smiled at him. "The government pays a bounty on wolves and coyotes and so forth. Well, I feel like a trapper after someone has caught a wolverine that's been robbing his line. You two are certainly entitled to a reward for catching Gold Brick."

Scott gulped. There seemed to be nothing he wanted to say that he could put into words. He shot a glance at Jack's shining face. His friend had struck it rich, after all. As for himself—he could be sure of starting University now.

But a disturbing thought still kept coming to the surface of Scott's mind. How about the mine? Placer pay-streaks often played out in two or three years. There should be something tangible to look forward to that would take the place of the elusive gold.

"I'll keep on planning," Scott said to himself. "If my asbestos turns out to be as good as it looks, Dad won't ever have to worry about finding new pay-streaks."

19

SCOTT MAKES UP HIS MIND

"D AD and Lars didn't get excited about my asbestos samples," Scott told Jack next morning. "Said there are showings of asbestos 'fluff' all through these mountains. I can hardly wait to hear what Dr. Lawson thinks about it."

The constable had already left in his own boat with his prisoner. Five of Gee-gee's best horses were whinnying and stamping around in the clearing behind the buildings. Antoin was bellowing, "Come on, Jack! I must follow close behind the policeman's boat. Perhaps Gold Brick will try to put water in the constable's gas." Antoin laughed deep down in his throat. "By gee! You boys were smart to catch that crook! *Au revoir,* Scott!"

Jack grinned. "That was more than 'fluff' you found, Scott. It was a whole mountain of asbestos. Good luck and s' long for now."

Scott waved farewell to his friend and the big riverman as they started down the trail to the river, with Dinty pacing close beside Jack. Then he turned to help

Gee-gee with the job of packing the two horses that were to carry the camp gear and dunnage.

"Fine weather, right enough," Gee-gee grunted as he hoisted up a pack. "Dunno as that airyplane will ever get here, though. Snow clouds'll be rollin' in around the mountains this time o' year."

Scott frowned as he cinched the diamond-hitch. He didn't want to think of the possibility of the weather closing in. It wasn't the prospect of being late for school opening that worried him—it was the possibility of not getting a chance to show his sample to Dr. Lawson.

That night the travelers camped at the canyon and, before noon next day, they reached the shore of Summit Lake. The sun was still shining and they had scarcely finished pitching the tent when Mr. Haliburton called out, "Listen!" And looking above the hills at the far end of the lake, Scott saw a black dot in the sky that grew larger and larger.

Three times the plane roared back and forth over their camp—lower each time, until they could see the black letters on its yellow wings and the pontoons shining like silver in the sunshine. Then it touched the water and the hills trembled as the pilot gunned the engine to nose gently into the gravel beach.

Dr. Lawson slid out of the cabin door and walked sure-footedly along a pontoon and jumped ashore. He greeted Mr. Haliburton briefly, shot a friendly glance at Scott, and strode over to the camp and picked up the ax. The boy watched with admiration while the tall, lean man felled a couple of small pines and neatly trimmed off the branches to make rollers to go under the pontoons.

"Golly!" Scott said to himself, "who would ever think of a man who can handle an ax like that having 'doctor' in front of his name."

"Moose meat for lunch, fine!" Dr. Lawson made himself at home around the campfire. "Well—how's it going, Dave? Having trouble with boulders? What does the gravel you're working in now look like?" The geologist had a score of questions to ask about the mine. Then he wanted to know, "What sort of a riverman is this Antoin? What size loads have they been hauling over the portage? Do you think they could use a bigger boat on the Dease?"

The questions seemed endless. It didn't take Scott long to realize that Dr. Lawson was no "stuffed shirt" who had knowledge only of what he had learned from his textbooks. Here was somebody who was interested in everything and everybody. His mind wasn't buried in old channels like Lars's.

The geologist's questions about the mine re-awakened in the boy a keen desire to know the whys and wherefores of things. What minerals had spouted up from under the earth in the early dawn of time? How had the mountains been formed? How and where had the great ice sheets of the glacial age affected them? That was the real mystery of the mountains—more exciting—more interesting than Gold Brick's petty scheming.

When Scott brought out his rock samples, the graying geologist had eyes only for the green-gold of the serpentine fragments. His eyebrows raised a little as he shredded a piece into white threads between his thumb and forefinger.

"This looks like true 'long-fibre' asbestos. With a high-way coming into the country, it could be valuable if there is enough of it."

"There's lots of it!" Scott spoke quietly to conceal his excitement. "The whole mountainside is white with it. I made a sketch-map—look!"

Dr. Lawson studied the map carefully. *"Hm-m-m!* You've got your head screwed on the right way, by the looks of things. This is a mighty good job for a field sketch!"

Scott flushed slightly. "I may be a bit out in my distances," he said. "And . . . and . . . Dad and Lars tell me there are showings of asbestos 'fluff' all through these mountains."

"They're right there," Dr. Lawson said gravely, "and so far none of them have been worth a second look. But I'd like to see this outcropping for myself. Let's see . . . it will be about ten miles from here." He turned to Scott's father. "Dave, I'm going to leave the report on your mine till next spring. We'll take the horses tomorrow morning and look over this serpentine your son has found."

At noon next day they were wading ankle-deep in the "mountain wool." The snowstorms foretold by Gee-gee had held off for another day at least and the golden sunshine was reflected in the faces of Dr. Lawson and Mr. Haliburton.

Dr. Lawson took bearings with his pocket compass and ranged far up the mountainside to chip off samples of rock. He made many entries in his notebook. And then, as they worked their way back toward the horses at timberline, his face glowed with a youthful enthusiasm that belied his graying hair.

"There's thousands of tons of it! The white stuff you see is only what has weathered out of the rock above. These are wide seams on the surface that could easily be broken up with air-hammers. Then the stuff could be poured down chutes into the valley. Of course, there'll have to be a road built to connect with the new highway —but that will come. Three years—or four years from now, you'll see a town built here."

Scott felt as though he were riding on air as they jogged back to camp. When they arrived, Dr. Lawson announced, "A find like you've made calls for a real blowout. Let's see what's in this crate of fresh stuff on the plane. Hah! Lettuce, celery, green onions, cucumbers and tomatoes! I'll whip up one of my special salads."

Perishable foods like that wouldn't stand the long river trip into Osprey Creek. It was two months since Scott had tasted such things. Their fresh tang began to make his mouth water. He couldn't wait for Dr. Lawson's elaborate preparations. There were other things in the crate, too. Scott slipped out of the tent with half a dozen bananas and a huge slice of watermelon.

He found Gee-gee sitting alone, poking at the embers of the campfire. Poor old Gee-gee! Scott could sympathize with him. All the things the old wrangler referred to contemptuously as new-fangled were coming to the Cassiar. Planes . . . highways . . . even new towns.

Scott unclasped his knife. "Have a slice of watermelon."

"Thank ye!"

With melon juice trickling from his ears to his chin, Scott mumbled, "Ought to buy some trucks, Gee-gee . . . lots of business for 'em when the highway comes through."

Gee-gee chuckled and spat out a mouthful of melon seeds.

"Wouldn't I look foolish drivin' a stinkin' truck? No siree! I'm stakin' a claim on that mountain that'll make me enough to buy some more hosses. Mebbe I'll have to blaze some new trails. There'll always be folks wantin' to push on beyond the end o' the road."

Things are going to work out for everyone, Scott thought as he went back into the tent. The watermelon and bananas hadn't dulled the edge of his appetite. He tucked in three heaping platefuls of the salad.

Dr. Lawson seemed as happy as an old dog who'd just had his ears scratched. "I'm sure you've found something big," he told Scott. "Asbestos is in great demand these days. And it's different from any other mineral. There are no deep shafts to be sunk to get it out and it doesn't have to go through any expensive smelting or refining process. The rock just has to be crushed and then the fibres are carded and spun into yarn like wool."

Scott realized how fortunate he'd been. It was more or less by blind luck that he had investigated the "wool that belongs mountain." Yet, if he hadn't had the initiative to make the map—then Dr. Lawson probably wouldn't have bothered to look at his discovery.

Next morning, as Scott walked down to board the plane, he said, "Dad, that money from the nuggets will give me a good start at University, won't it?"

His father nodded.

"And then," Scott went on, "I can get summer work with survey parties to pay my way. Later, perhaps when I'm in my last year, there might be money coming in from the asbestos claims."

Mr. Haliburton nodded again. "I don't think there's much doubt of that."

"Golly!" Scott beamed. "It will be a big help if I want to take post-graduate courses, won't it? Oh, boy! I'll bet you'll be proud of me when I can write 'doctor' in front of my name like Dr. Lawson!"

Dave Haliburton smiled as his hand gripped Scott's shoulder. "I certainly will, Son. But, don't ever forget, it will take a lot more than money to make you Dr. Haliburton! First and foremost, it will take a lot of hard work. Never forget that!"

"I won't forget," Scott promised as he climbed into the plane.

Minutes later, the pontoons had lifted from the water and mountains seemed to be floating all about him. The white square of the tent soon disappeared and ahead the black strip of a river twisted and turned and dwindled into a narrow thread among rounded peaks wrapped in clouds. Turbulent air currents started to jar the plane with sledge-hammer blows.

Puffs of cloud streaked past the windows at sickening speed. Had Gee-gee been right about the weather? Were they going to have to turn back, after all? The plane dropped sharply in a down draft and Manty shivered and whined. Scott reached down and held a front paw.

The dog gratefully licked his hand. The boy burped and made a solemn resolution never again to mix watermelon, bananas, celery and green onions.

For twenty minutes the plane pitched and rocked in the turbulence. Below them, through the snow squalls, the occupants caught occasional glimpses of bare rock and dwarf trees. Then, at last, they were gliding smoothly southward over the sun-bathed valley of a large river.

Scott said to himself, "We've made it! It won't be long now. First thing I'll do when we get to the railway is write a note to Jack to tell him the asbestos is something really big."

Dr. Lawson was bellowing in his ear. "We're through the pass—that's the Finlay, one of the headwaters of the Peace River, we're following now. Those are the Rockies on the left—hundreds and hundreds of mountains —who knows how many of them hide a mystery like your asbestos? It'll take young men—young men with know-how and stamina to find out."

Scott smiled to himself as he let go of Manty's paw and stroked the dog's sleek, black fur. His mind was made up now. He was going to be one of those young men.

WILLIAM G. CRISP

was born in Dawson City in the Canadian Yukon, grew up in Vancouver, British Columbia, and eventually headed north as radio operator in a trading schooner bound, via Bering Straits, for a three-year cruise in Arctic waters. During the ice-bound winters his duties ranged from sending out weather reports to running fish nets under the ice to provide food for the post dog team. He raised and trained a team of seven huskies and used them on sled trips to visit the "neighbors"—fifty to one hundred and fifty miles along the coast.

Dogs were still being used to haul the winter mail when William Crisp was transferred as a Hudson's Bay Company trading post manager to the vast, mountainous Cassiar district in northwestern British Columbia. He spent two winters at Dease Lake, which is frozen from October to June. At this post he had as a pet and hunting companion a small dog, native to the Tahltan Indian country, that had been trained to corner bears in the spring when the crust on the snow was strong enough to support a small dog, but not sufficient to keep a large animal from breaking through. It was inevitable that one of these "Bear Dogs" should appear in his *White Gold in the Cassiar,* first prize winner of the *Boys' Life—Dodd, Mead Prize Competition.*

Amateur radio has been one of William Crisp's hobbies since his school days. During the fifteen years he spent in the north, radio kept him in touch with civilization. After circumstances compelled him to move to the southern part of the province—and become the property of a wire-haired terrier instead of a Tahltan Bear Dog—his "ham" station meant that he did not lose touch with the north.